# EVEREST

**A world of adventure from
Gordon Korman**

# EVEREST

# ISLAND

www.scholastic.com

www.gordonkorman.com

# GORDON KORMAN

## BOOK TWO: THE CLIMB

# EVEREST

AN
**APPLE**
PAPERBACK

SCHOLASTIC INC.
New York  Toronto  London  Auckland  Sydney
Mexico City  New Delhi  Hong Kong  Buenos Aires

ISBN 0-439-40506-8

12 11 10 9 8 7 6 5 4          2 3 4 5 6 7/0

Printed in the U.S.A.          40

First Scholastic printing, September 2002

For Mark Wise, M.D.,
expert on what ails you
at twenty-nine thousand feet

# PROLOGUE

Dominic Alexis was waiting his turn to use the airplane bathroom when he got his first glimpse of Mount Everest.

Standing there in the narrow aisle of the 747, he froze, gawking out the porthole in the emergency door. To the north rose the jagged, icy spires of the Himalayas, the highest mountain range on the face of the earth. And right in the heart of it, the giant among giants — barely lower than the cruising altitude of the plane — Everest.

*There should be trumpets,* he thought reverently. *A fanfare. Fireworks.*

Norman "Tilt" Crowley came up behind Dominic and hip-checked him out of the way. "Man, this airline stinks! What do you have to do to get a bag of peanuts?"

Wordlessly, Dominic pointed out the window at the unmistakable silhouette.

Tilt peered through the porthole. "Big deal — Mount Everest. What, you thought they were going to move it before we got here?"

But for all his attitude, Tilt stayed riveted to the

spot, fascinated by the sight of the big mountain that the Nepalese called *Jongmalungma* — "Goddess, Mother of the World."

An announcement came from the cockpit. "On our left, we see Mount Everest." It was repeated in several other languages.

There was a rush for the left side of the plane. For most of the passengers, this was the closest they would come to the top of the world. But Dominic and Tilt were part of SummitQuest, the youngest expedition ever to attempt the planet's highest peak. For them, the massive profile of Everest was the shape of things to come.

Sammi Moon shut off her Walkman and rushed over to join them at the porthole. "How is it? Extreme, right?" She spotted the mountain. "It's beautiful!"

"You paint it; I'll climb it," put in Tilt. "That lump of rock is going to make me famous."

"We have to wake Perry," said Dominic. "He should see this."

The fourth member of their team, Perry Noonan, was in his seat, fast asleep.

"Are you kidding?" snorted Tilt. "He's so scared of Everest that he can't even face the picture in the in-flight magazine. He'd take one look out the window and wet his pants!"

Dominic's eyes never left the mountain. "You're crazy if you're not a little bit scared."

"I'm just amped," said Sammi. "I can't believe we're really on our way!"

They squinted through the clouds, trying to discern the summit — the object of years of climbing and months of preparation.

What Dominic, Tilt, Sammi, and Perry could not know was that the mist-obscured peak was more than a goal. For one of the four team members, it would be a final resting place.

THE CLIMB

# CHAPTER ONE

Kathmandu Airport, Nepal. Passports, permits, and paperwork.

The arrivals line stretched from gate 1 to gate B76.

Cap Cicero, legendary mountaineer and expedition leader, marched his team straight through in five minutes.

No one questioned this. Their sponsor was Summit Athletic, one of the richest corporations in the world. Big money opened a lot of doors and smoothed a lot of paths.

"So long, suckers," Tilt tossed over his shoulder at the milling, exasperated crowd they'd left behind in the passport queue. He awarded Perry a slap on the back of the head. "Tell your uncle I said thanks."

Perry's uncle Joe Sullivan was the president and founder of Summit Athletic. Although Cicero would never admit it publicly, that was the only reason Perry was on the team. No one believed this more strongly than Perry himself.

The red-haired boy sighed, wishing he was al-

EVEREST

most anywhere else in the world than Nepal. "Yeah, when Summit does something, they do it right."

"You think they'll have limos for us?" Tilt asked hopefully.

But when the group passed through the gate, their welcome consisted of a hand-lettered sign scribbled in Magic Marker on the flap of a corrugated box:

SUMIT

Dominic regarded the short, squat man holding up the cardboard. "Is that a Sherpa?" he whispered to Cicero. Sherpas are the inhabitants of the Khumbu region around Everest.

Cicero roared like a bull moose and rushed forward to throw his arms around the man with the sign.

"This isn't a Sherpa!" he cried. "It's *the* Sherpa! I want you to meet Babu Pemba, the greatest climbing Sherpa the mountain has ever seen!"

"*Climbing* Sherpa?" Tilt stared at the chubby Babu, who was taking bites out of a large sandwich clenched in his free hand. "Isn't he a little, you know, out of shape?"

THE CLIMB

Babu surprised him by replying in perfect English with only a slight accent, "Oh, no. I'm just short for my weight."

Sammi giggled until she had the hiccups. Even Perry cracked a smile.

"I've heard of you," Dominic said with respect. "You saved Cap's life on Annapurna." He indicated the sandwich. "Is that a traditional Sherpa delicacy?"

"Philly cheese steak," mumbled Babu, his mouth full. He looked meaningfully from Dominic to Cicero. The message was clear. Tilt, while only fourteen years old, was built like a lumberjack and radiated power and physical ability. Perry and Sammi, at fifteen, were both solidly put together. But Dominic Alexis looked like a fifth grader. He'd just turned thirteen and was small for his age. Who in his right mind would bring him on an Everest ascent?

Cicero answered the unspoken question. "He climbs bigger than he looks."

It was a measure of their respect for each other that the Sherpa accepted this completely and without comment.

Babu Pemba drove them to their hotel in a rented Volkswagen bus so ancient that pieces were flaking off as they rattled over the cobblestones and rutted pavement. The chaos on the streets was total. There were cars and trucks that made the VW look like a brand-new Ferrari. Motorcycles and mopeds whizzed everywhere. Further down the food chain, bicycles and rickshaws did their best to compete against the motorized vehicles. Yaks and other beasts of burden meandered along like they owned the place. Flocks of geese were driven in all directions. There seemed to be no traffic regulations. The rule was every yak for itself.

To four teenagers who had never left the United States, Kathmandu was an eye-opener. Dilapidated hovels stood next to modern hotels and Buddhist temples. The air reeked of car exhaust, incense, and manure. The food smells were positively bizarre. The general din was a mixture of unmuffled motors, religious chants, animal lowing, and rock music. Orange-clad monks walked the streets side by side with businessmen, panhandlers, and Western tourists.

At the hotel, the SummitQuest group met up with Andrea Oberman, the expedition doctor, and Lenny "Sneezy" Tkakzuk, the cameraman who would be recording the ascent for the Summit Athletic Web site. Both were top-notch climbing guides.

THE CLIMB

**8**

That completed the team — four adults and four teens. If one of the young climbers succeeded in reaching the summit, he or she would break the record currently held by the Z-man, Ethan Zaph, and become the youngest human ever to conquer Everest.

# CHAPTER TWO

An expedition survives on its supplies. That was Cicero's job while in Kathmandu — to make sure SummitQuest had all its material and personnel in place when the climbers arrived at Base Camp eleven days later. Everest Base Camp had nothing — no year-round inhabitants, no stores, no conveniences. Everything there was shipped from home, sent by yak train from Kathmandu, or purchased in one of the villages on the trek.

As the guides set about seeing to the arrangements, Cicero had this warning for his young team: "I'm not going to be a hypocrite about this. If I can trust you to take on Everest, I can trust you to kill a few hours in Kathmandu. Don't talk to strangers, stay close to the hotel, and keep out of trouble."

Sammi sprung up from the lumpy couch in the hotel lobby. "Time to see the world."

Cicero looked disgusted. "Can you at least wait till I'm out of the building before you completely disregard everything I say?"

"Come on, who's with me?" Sammi persisted.

"There's nothing to see in Kathmandu," Tilt assured her. "This town is a sewer." And he headed for the hotel's seedy basement rec room to play video games.

In the end, Sammi headed out alone. Dominic left, too, but in a different direction. He wandered for a long time, barely noticing the wild and noisy activity of the city streets. He saw only the footsteps of legendary climbers on the worn cobblestones. Most of the great Himalayan expeditions had started right here.

His reverie was interrupted by a half-demented scream. "Get out of the way! *Get out of the way!*"

Sammi flashed into his field of vision and right out again, a blur on rented Rollerblades. He could follow her progress down the sloped street, not by watching her, but by noting the pattern made by people jumping out of her path.

Dominic allowed himself a small smile. That was Sammi. She was not so much a pure climber as an all-purpose daredevil. Everest appealed to her because it was, as she put it, "extreme."

He found what he was looking for right where the guidebook said it would be — a small Buddhist temple sandwiched between a dry cleaner and a shop that sold junky souvenirs to tourists. He stepped into the tiny courtyard, and the sounds of the city seemed to fade away. Himalayan climbers had great respect for the traditions of Buddhism, the religion of their Sherpa guides.

This was not a large temple or even an important one. But it was close to the hotel district and had been mentioned in some of the books Dominic had read. Cap Cicero had come here before his first Everest ascent. So had Sir Edmund Hillary.

He slipped off his shoes and approached the prayer wheels. Spinning them was thought to release the blessings heavenward. He hesitated, unsure of what was expected of him. He didn't want to do something stupid and offend an ancient religion.

A quiet voice behind him said, "You just turn them. There's no right way or wrong way." A tall figure came into view and stood beside him.

Dominic recognized the face instantly. "You're Ethan Zaph!"

The young man looked surprised. "Do I know you?"

"I followed your climb last year inch by inch on the Internet! I kept a scrapbook with all the pictures from the paper. When you hit the summit, my brother and I were going nuts!"

Ethan grinned. "Me, too. You guys climbers?"

"Big-time!" Dominic exclaimed. "My brother's climbed with you. Chris Alexis?"

THE CLIMB

Ethan nodded. "Oh, sure, I know Chris. He's here, right? With the Cap Cicero expedition? I was almost on that team."

"Chris isn't here," said Dominic in a subdued tone. "He didn't make the cut."

Ethan was shocked. "Chris Alexis is the best climber I know! Why would Cap cut him?"

"When you quit SummitQuest," Dominic explained, "Summit decided to go for your record. Chris is too old to beat your mark, so they filled the team with younger kids — like me." He held out his hand. "I'm Dominic."

Ethan made no move to take it. "Like you? You're going up that mountain? How old are you — ten?"

"Thirteen," replied Dominic, a little defensively.

"Has Cap gone crazy? Is everybody on the team like you?"

"I'm the youngest," Dominic admitted. "And the smallest. But Cap knows what he's doing."

"Does he?" Ethan challenged. "That's a mean mountain! When I summited, I came back twenty-three pounds lighter, dehydrated, and with three separated ribs from coughing!"

Dominic took a half-step back, his shoulder brushing up against the prayer wheels. "It's really nice meeting you. I hope we get the chance to climb together someday."

It was Ethan's turn to retreat. "Listen, I'm sure you've got talent. It runs in the family. Just do me one favor, okay? Go slow, and be honest with yourself about when it's time to quit. There are a lot of dead people up there. You don't want to be one of them."

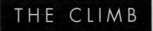

THE CLIMB

# CHAPTER THREE

At six o'clock the next morning, the Summit-Quest team piled themselves and their luggage inside the Volkswagen bus.

"Hold it." Dr. Oberman took a close look at Sammi. She had a swollen lip and a nasty scratch across her chin. "What happened to you?"

Sammi shrugged sheepishly. "You should see the other guy."

Cicero jumped on this. "You got into a fight in Kathmandu?"

"I was Rollerblading and I hit a yak," Sammi confessed.

"Those things are tougher than they look," put in Babu, who was munching on an Egg McMuffin and holding two more in reserve.

Soon they arrived at a small military airfield outside of town. There, waiting on the tarmac, was a decrepit-looking army surplus helicopter from the Korean War. Parts of it were held together with duct tape.

"That," said Tilt, "is never going to get off the ground."

EVEREST

It did, though, promptly at seven, with a roar that threatened to jar Tilt's back teeth loose. The pilot, who spoke no English, had handed out cotton balls for them to use as earplugs. No one had bothered. They were bothering now.

There were no seats. Tilt perched on his duffel bag, hanging on to a frayed leather strap on the wall.

*God, this country is a sinkhole*, he raged inwardly. And this had to be first class, because Summit always paid for the very best. Pity the poor saps who were doing this on the cheap.

*But you're here*, he reminded himself. *And every day takes you closer to the summit.*

The chance to conquer Everest had become the center of Tilt's universe. The others were hobby climbers; for Tilt this was serious business. Ethan Zaph was famous, with six figures in his college account, thanks to last year's expedition. Well, if Ethan could get rich from an ascent at fifteen, then it stood to reason that Tilt could get even richer at fourteen. He'd endorse ice axes and crampons in climbing magazines. His face would appear on cereal boxes. His future was sitting there, just waiting to be claimed. All he had to do was get up one mountain.

Not that he was going to get any help from his teammates. Cicero had a big name, but he

was past his prime. And anyway, it would take all his talents just to keep the others from killing themselves. Dr. Oberman was all doctor, no climber. Sneezy cared about his video camera, period. And Babu? Hah! Baboon would be more like it. The guy was 90 percent lard. He couldn't get up Everest unless someone told him there was a pizza waiting at the top!

The country they were passing over was green and hilly and dotted with tiny villages. To Tilt, they all looked like a few miserable shacks arranged around a gas station that had long since gone out of business.

The farther they got from Kathmandu, the more primitive the construction became — mud huts. This place was like something out of *The Flintstones!*

While the helicopter always seemed to be the same distance from the ground, it was pretty clear that the general direction was up. Tilt could tell from the popping of his ears and by glances at Perry's three-thousand-dollar climber's watch — another gift from his rich uncle, along with his place on this team. They had started at 4,120 feet, and now the altimeter was approaching nine thousand.

The flight lasted two earsplitting hours. Their destination was indistinguishable from all the miles they had passed over — a depressing, dingy, dirt-poor village amid acres of terraced barley fields.

Five minutes later, they were standing with their knapsacks, holding their ears as the chopper roared away. Sneezy videotaped it disappearing over the bleak horizon.

Perry looked around. "Where's Mount Everest?"

Cicero laughed in his face. "Fourteen hours on a plane, but I guess nobody had any time to read the material I handed out. Everest is like Disneyland, Noonan. This is where we wait for the courtesy van to take us to Base Camp."

Perry kept his mouth shut. How had it come to this? He was on the wrong side of the globe and soon he would be on Everest itself! And all because he didn't have the guts to disappoint Uncle Joe.

Joe Sullivan. Was it that the man always got what he wanted because he was a billionaire? Or was he a billionaire because he always got what he wanted? It didn't matter. Right now he wanted his favorite nephew up Mount Everest. What that nephew wanted was apparently much less important.

Perry sighed. He hadn't expected to make this team, so he had done no Himalayan research at all. The Disneyland explanation was clearly not the truth, but he had no way of knowing what was.

Dominic, who had read every word he could get his hands on about Everest, pointed to the northeast. "If this village is Lukla, then Base Camp should be about thirty-five miles that way."

"But how do we get there?" asked Perry.

"We walk," Cicero replied.

Perry just stared.

Dr. Oberman took pity on him and explained. "The problem isn't the thirty-five miles; it's the altitude. We're now at nine thousand feet, and Base Camp is almost twice that. If you go up too fast, the changes in atmospheric pressure and the thinning of the air could make you sick and even kill you. At minimum, it would scuttle your chances of ever attempting the mountain."

"It's called acclimatization," Sneezy supplied. "If you could beam somebody from sea level to the summit of Everest, he'd be dead in three minutes. The air there has two-thirds less oxygen. That's why we have to go up slowly."

"How slowly?" Tilt asked suspiciously.

"Ten days," said Cicero. "That's to Base Camp at seventeen thousand six hundred feet. Acclimatizing on the mountain is a little trickier."

"Ten days?" Sammi was distraught. "Ten days

around *here*? I mean, it's okay, but there's not exactly a ton of excitement."

Babu brayed a laugh right into her face. "Sure there is," the stout Sherpa guffawed. "Wait until you see the bathrooms!"

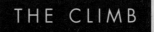

# CHAPTER FOUR

http://www.summathletic.com/everest/
trek

Day 3: Trekking north along the *Dudh Kosi*, or "Milky River," the four youngest Everesters of all time have traveled for a week, including three rest days to get used to the altitude. Each step takes them farther into the land of the giants.

The names defy pronunciation: Kangtega, Thomserku, Ama Dablam. **CLICK HERE** to see the climbers hiking before the immense granite wall of Nuptse, a Himalayan Hoover Dam, four miles in the sky. It is from behind these multipeaked ramparts that Everest will finally reveal itself, the titan among titans.

This is the payoff for their arduous journey: multicolored strings of Buddhist prayer flags, carved Mani stones, and the most spectacular peaks on the planet. Nothing could be so exhilarating.

EVEREST

"I'm *bored*," Sammi complained. "What say we find a flat log and shoot some of those rapids on the Dudh Kosi?"

Dr. Oberman was horrified. "That's glacial runoff! If you fall in that frigid water, you'll be dead faster than the passengers on the *Titanic*!"

"Well, how about we jog for a while?" she suggested. "Get to Base Camp a couple of days early."

The doctor shook her head. "We have to take it slow. If we ascend too fast, we'll risk altitude sickness."

"If we stay here, we'll risk lapsing into a coma," Sammi countered.

The guides struggled to dig up some entertainment. It was a lost cause. Their "hotels" were little more than dormitory-style huts. Shopping was out because there was virtually nothing to buy. They toured villages that could be experienced in thirty seconds. Monasteries took longer, but Perry turned out to be allergic to the incense. It was brutal.

Sammi had always craved adrenaline — even before she was old enough to understand the word. At age four she had leaped a line of wastebaskets while riding a bicycle that still had training wheels. Broken her ankle, too, taking the pain without so much as a single tear.

THE CLIMB

Along with Caleb, her boyfriend and partner in crime, she had tried it all — extreme rock climbing, extreme skateboarding, extreme ski jumping, and much, much more. But this was the toughest of them all.

Extreme boredom.

Tilt crouched in the tiny foyer, pounding the keyboard of his laptop computer, which was hooked up to E-mail via SummitQuest's satellite phone.

**E-mail Message**
**TO: bv@national-daily.com**
**SUBJECT: Arrived in Dingboche**

**We've been running into a lot of climbers from other expeditions on the trek, and everybody says the same thing: Dominic Alexis is too young and too small to take on Everest. Sure, I'm only a year and a half older, but I'm a foot taller and almost double his weight. Ask anybody here — Cap should have his head examined for picking a shrimp like that for the team. . . .**

Tilt was under secret contract to provide inside details of the SummitQuest expedition to the *National Daily*. It was a dangerous arrangement, no doubt about it. If Cicero found out, he'd kick Tilt off the team in a heartbeat. But how else was a guy supposed to pay for his ice ax and crampons and climbing harness? For state-of-the-art Gore-Tex clothing? He couldn't take on Everest with secondhand junk financed by a paper route. He felt a little guilty about spying on everybody, but he needed the money. Not everybody had a billionaire uncle, after all.

His reports were basically just a lot of gossip. Sammi E-mailed her boyfriend back home every three seconds. Perry was only here because of his uncle. Cicero was a control freak with a short fuse.

But lately Tilt's attention had settled on one teammate and one only — Dominic.

His thinking was simple. Tilt's entire future depended on making it to the top of Everest. Only two things could spoil that plan. 1) He might not get there, and 2) Dominic might get there with him.

The problem was that Dominic was younger than Tilt. If the shrimp summited, *he*, and not Tilt, would become the new Ethan Zaph. The record

THE CLIMB

— and fame and fortune — would go to Dominic.

Of course, there was no way a ninety-pound runt was going to climb the highest peak on the planet. But why take the chance? If the *National Daily* kept printing articles about how unsafe it was for Dominic to be on the mountain, there could be a public outcry to ground him. Who knows — Dominic's own parents might even yank him.

Tilt continued to type:

**If Dominic gets into trouble up there, it'll risk all our chances for the summit. And if he gets killed, it'll be a black eye for the whole country of Nepal, who will look like idiots for letting Cap put a little kid on his climbing permit. . . .**

"There you are," came a voice.

Shocked, Tilt jumped to his feet to find Dominic in the tiny entranceway. "Get out of here, shrimp!"

Dominic peered at the screen. "What are you writing?"

In a single motion, Tilt slammed the laptop shut and swung it like a battle-ax, smacking

Dominic in the chin. "None of your business!"

The impact sent Dominic staggering backward. His small knapsack dropped from his shoulder and hit the floor. He stood there, coughing into his fist. The Khumbu cough, Dr. Oberman called it. Caused by the altitude and the thin, dry air. Sneezy and Perry had it, too.

"I was E-mailing my dad," Tilt lied. The kid was likely to run crying to Cicero. That would mean trouble. "It was private. Sorry."

"Cap says we're ready to roll," Dominic managed between spasms.

"Gotcha." Tilt stuffed the laptop into his own pack. "You sound lousy, shrimp. It's hard enough to sleep around here with Sneezy and Perry barking up a storm. Now it's going to be like feeding time at the dog pound."

"I'm okay," said Dominic.

But he did not feel okay. The cough had come with a scatterbrained, spacey feeling. It had taken him fifteen minutes to stuff a couple of T-shirts and a few toiletries into his knapsack. It should have been a thirty-second operation. Yet for some reason, it had seemed as complicated as defusing a bomb.

Tilt tucked the laptop under his arm. "Let's go."

His pack forgotten, Dominic followed.

THE CLIMB

"Hey, stupid — " The big boy soccer-kicked the knapsack out of the hut, and the two hurried after it.

The true monsters revealed themselves during the day's trek. Lhotse was first, the fourth-highest mountain on Earth, towering in mighty profile behind the Nuptse wall. Another quarter mile up the trail, the pinnacle of Everest came into view.

It was a view Dominic had been waiting for his entire life. But now, slogging along in a half-daze, he just couldn't seem to bring himself to care.

As the trail wound higher, the air was becoming increasingly thin. He found himself gasping for breath on a path he would have had no problem sprinting back home near sea level.

His cough was getting worse. It was no longer the dry hacking of the others. Each bronchitis-like spasm seemed to be coming from deep in his chest.

By noon, they had reached the heap of stones that marked the Khumbu glacier's terminal moraine.

"Terminal," Perry repeated aloud. Around here, even the innocent words sounded deadly.

"Moraine means any debris pushed by the glacier," Cicero explained. "It's just a whole lot of rocks and dirt, because, at sixteen thousand feet, there are no trees or anything green. We're on the moon, guys. Or as close as you can get without a rocket."

Dominic forged on, choking and wheezing. He found himself looking down in intense concentration as he trudged over the rocks and chunks of glacial ice that littered the snow-packed trail.

In the back of his mind, alarm bells were going off: *You've made it up every crag and cliff in the East! This shouldn't be so hard!*

Late in the afternoon, the group turned off the trail to the tiny village of Lobuche. Cicero sent Babu to secure the team sleeping accommodations for the next two nights.

"Two more nights?" Sammi was distraught. "But Base Camp is only a few miles away!"

"Last stop," the expedition leader promised. "A couple of nights above sixteen thousand and you'll be ready for base."

"We're ready *now*," Tilt argued. "We've been on this dumb trail forever. . . ."

He fell silent, realizing that no one was paying attention. All eyes were on Dominic, who was still trudging along the path. If the boy had any idea that he was alone, he gave no indication.

"Hey, kid!" called Cicero. Louder: "Dominic, come back!"

THE CLIMB

His youngest climber did not even look up.

Sammi rushed over and got Dominic turned around. He took three steps and collapsed, sinking to a sitting position on the trekking route.

Cicero was there in a heartbeat, posing the questions that decades of Himalayan experience had made automatic: "Feeling dizzy, kid? Can't get your act together? Do the simplest little things seem like rocket science?"

Dr. Oberman clued in. "You think he's got HAPE?" she asked in alarm.

"But we're not even in Base Camp!" Dominic managed to protest.

"Listen to his lungs," ordered Cicero.

She produced a stethoscope from the medical pack and held the bell to Dominic's chest. There was a breathless silence.

"What's HAPE?" Perry whispered to Sneezy.

"High Altitude Pulmonary Edema," the guide replied grimly. "Altitude sickness."

The doctor exhaled nervously. "Fluid on the lungs. It's HAPE, all right."

# CHAPTER FIVE

*It's like being dead*, thought Dominic.

He was lying flat on his back in a Gamow bag at the Himalayan Rescue Association clinic in the village of Pheriche, several miles south and two thousand feet below Lobuche. The vinyl bag billowed around him as Dr. Drake of the clinic pumped air inside — the thing was a cross between a coffin and an inflatable life raft. Through the clear plastic window, he could see Cicero and Dr. Oberman peering in at him in concern. He felt like a lab rat.

No, that was wrong. The indignity of the bag paled before larger, more disturbing truths: *I am halfway around the world from my home and family. I have a potentially life-threatening illness. . . .*

That was probably a little too dramatic. Most people recovered from HAPE. A few of them even went on to climb the mountain. It was unlikely, but not impossible. He could be one of those.

*If Cap and Andrea will even let me try.*

The letdown hurt worse than the edema. He

couldn't shake the feeling that his Everest dreams were over.

Was the bag working? He couldn't tell. The pumped-in air increased atmospheric pressure, which simulated lower altitude. The clinic was at fourteen thousand feet, but the altimeter on his watch read 7,487. He certainly felt clearer-headed. But he was still coughing.

The discomfort and claustrophobia were nothing compared to the agony of not knowing.

*Come on, Cap! Don't send me home.*

Finally, he was allowed to crawl out of the bag. He was examined by Dr. Drake and then by Dr. Oberman. Cicero sent him outside to await his fate.

"He's okay, right?" Dr. Oberman asked the other doctor. "Full recovery?"

"You caught the illness early enough," Dr. Drake confirmed. "I'd say full recovery, but who knows? I've never treated a thirteen-year-old before."

"You're kidding," said Cicero.

"The Sherpa children are born to the altitude, and none of the expeditions ever bring kids along." He looked at Cicero. "Why did *you?*"

"That kid is one of the toughest climbers I've ever seen," Cicero said readily.

Dr. Drake was appalled. "He's a *climber?* An *Everest* climber?"

"He looks little — " Cicero shrugged. "Okay, he *is* little. But he's got a mixture of spirit and ability this mountain hasn't seen in twenty years. In Alaska, I watched him save a teammate on nothing but guts."

"Physically he's still a child," Dr. Drake insisted. "He was taking two steps to everyone else's one on the trek."

"My mistake, not his," Cicero conceded.

"And mine," Dr. Oberman added.

"He should go home," Dr. Drake said decisively "No, that's not strong enough. He never should have been here in the first place."

On the way out, Dr. Oberman drew a deep breath. "It's not going to be easy to break the news to Dominic."

The team leader grabbed her arm. "Don't say a word," he ordered. "If he asks, just say you're treating his HAPE, that's it. I don't want him to know he might still climb."

She gawked at him. "Climb? But Dr. Drake said — "

"Three times I tried to wash that kid out," Cicero interrupted. "And three times he proved me wrong. I'm not underestimating him again."

Base Camp was the biggest town the SummitQuest team had seen in a week. More than three hundred tents, big and small, dotted the boulder-strewn ice, and at least that many people — foreigners and Sherpas alike — bustled around, talking, laughing, testing equipment, and unloading shipments from an armada of laden yaks lumbering up the glacier.

The altitude was 17,600 feet, higher by half a mile than any peak in the lower forty-eight U.S. states.

Perry couldn't take his eyes off the beehive of activity. "I think we're going to need a bigger mountain."

"Don't worry," laughed Sneezy, who was filming the spectacle. "Most of these people are porters and Base Camp staff. We won't all be on the summit ridge at the same time."

"Don't forget cooks," added Babu, who had already helped himself to a cinnamon bun from the mess.

Under a huge banner strung across a boulder the size of a cement mixer, the Summit camp consisted of an enormous bright orange tent surrounded by four smaller two-person rigs for sleeping. The central structure was called the kitchen, but in reality, it was the living room, dining room, rec room, communications facility, and sleeping quarters for the Sherpas. Cicero had employed eight of them — four climbing Sherpas and four camp staff.

"Now, this is more like it!" exclaimed Tilt, dropping his pack and tossing himself onto an air mattress. After staying in a string of villages in which light and heat came from lamps and stoves fueled by burning dried yak droppings, the Summit encampment had all the comforts of home. Thanks to a solar generator, electricity powered lamps, a stereo, and even a TV and VCR.

By the time Sammi appeared at the flap, he had popped in a tape and was lost in the depths of *The Terminator*.

"Come on," she beckoned. "Let's take a look around."

"I'm busy."

Sammi rolled her eyes. "Tilt, you've got the greatest adventure on Earth right outside this tent."

He glared at her. "I've been living with the baboons for a week and a half. Go away. I want to watch Arnold Schwarzenegger shoot somebody!"

"Jerk," she muttered, and disappeared

The staccato chime of a telephone interrupted one of the movie's better killing sprees. He searched the cavernous tent, his eyes falling on the communications table — really a board propped on rocks.

He picked up the satellite phone. "Hello?"

"Who is this?" Cicero's voice. "Larry?"

"It's Tilt."

"Oh." The distaste was evident in the team leader's voice. Cicero didn't much care for Tilt, and the feeling was mutual. "Listen, tell Larry or Babu I'll be up there late tomorrow. Andrea's staying with Dominic. They'll be a few days behind me."

Tilt froze. "You mean Andrea will."

"And Dominic. They're taking it slow to make sure the HAPE doesn't come back."

"But — " Tilt had been privately celebrating Dominic's departure. "He's okay?"

"If he isn't, we'll just climb without him. You've got to be flexible in the Himalayas." A pause, then, "Tilt, this call costs five bucks a minute. If you've got something to say, say it."

"Well — isn't that kind of — you know — dangerous?"

Laughter brayed over the satellite phone. "Take a look out the tent flap, kid. That's Everest, not Gymboree."

"I mean extra dangerous for Dominic," Tilt stammered, "because he's so young — "

There was irritation on the other end of the

line. "Just tell Larry and Babu I'm on my way. Think you can handle that?"

Tilt bristled. "Yeah, I'll tell Sneezy — and Baboon." He slammed down the phone.

The cold sweat came almost immediately. Why did he do that? He had nothing to gain and everything to lose by getting on Cicero's nerves. Back in the States, his attitude had almost cost him a spot on the team.

He relaxed a little. The satellite connection was lousy and crackled with static. The team leader probably hadn't even heard. He had nothing to worry about.

*Besides,* thought Tilt, *I've got more important things to do.*

Twenty million *National Daily* readers needed to hear the story of how climbing legend Cap Cicero was recklessly risking the life of a thirteen-year-old.

He pulled out his laptop and booted it up.

# CHAPTER SIX

Base Camp was a land of logos — Summit, Nike, Coca-Cola, Starbucks. There were national expeditions, too, under bedsheet-sized flags. These ranged from a Japanese team twenty climbers strong to two affable brothers hoping to become the first Guamanians ever to scale the world's tallest peak.

*Guam. The beach. Sea level.* It sounded good to Perry.

Loud crashing from below made him jump. "What was that?"

Sammi laughed with delight. "We're on a glacier. It's a frozen river — always shifting and breaking apart." She did a dance to the beat of a series of aftershocks. "It's like Rice Krispies — snap, crackle, pop — "

"More like snap, crackle, heart attack," Perry said feelingly.

"It *is* pretty extreme," she chortled. "I can't believe Dominic's missing this."

Dominic. As soon as the news had come in that Dominic's life was no longer in danger,

EVEREST

Perry's jealousy had begun. The boy now had a built-in excuse not to climb.

"Look." Sammi pointed. "Ethan Zaph's team."

The famous Ethan was climbing with an expedition called This Way Up, which boasted the boldest plan on the mountain that year. After a punishing ascent of the 27,920-foot Lhotse, they would traverse to Everest via the South Col. Even more impressive, Ethan would be summiting both peaks without oxygen. All but the most elite mountaineers breathed bottled gas in the infamous Death Zone above twenty-five thousand feet. Yet Ethan, who was not yet seventeen, would be climbing without it — up not just one mountain, but two.

This Way Up's camp was even larger and more elaborate than SummitQuest's, sporting a library and even a makeshift shower. There was no sign of Ethan, but a tall, thin, olive-skinned young man with thick glasses was outside one of the smaller tents. He was painting a wooden sign that hung just above the flap:

> **NESTOR ALI**
> **FIRST-EVER NEARSIGHTED**
> **PUERTO RICAN/PAKISTANI**
> **DOUBLE ASCENT & YETI RECONNAISSANCE**

THE CLIMB

Perry frowned. "What's a 'yeti'?"

"Haven't you heard of the abominable snow-man?" Nestor asked pleasantly. "It's a local legend — kind of the Bigfoot of the Himalayas. He's got to be up there somewhere."

Sammi gave him a skeptical once-over. "Who else do you expect to find? The Tooth Fairy?"

It turned out that Nestor was a journalist who had been hired by an Internet magazine to write humorous articles about Everest. His job, essentially, was to make fun of everything. He had already dubbed the sea of corporate logos "McBase Camp." The expedition leaders were "Everest cruise directors."

"Where does the abominable snowman fit in?" asked Perry.

"Look around you," said Nestor. "Everybody has a gimmick. There's a guy on the Australian team who plans to be the first garbage collector to stand on the summit. The Peruvians are taking a lab rat up there — the first rodent on top of the world. On the other side of camp, there's a lady who wants to be the first great-grandmother to make it through the Khumbu Icefall. Why can't I be the yeti guy?"

"Watch it, Nestor," came a voice behind him. "I think you're talking to one of those gimmicks right now."

Ethan Zaph stepped through the tent flap, unfolding his six-foot-two-inch frame. He faced Sammi. "SummitQuest, right? And you want to be the youngest girl?"

"I don't care about records," Sammi told him. "I climb for the rush." She held out her hand. "Sammi Moon. I'm a fan — but that doesn't mean I won't smoke your butt on the mountain. Carrot-top here is Perry Noonan."

There were handshakes all around.

"So you're after my record," Ethan said to Perry. "No, wait — what happened to Chris Alexis's brother?"

"He had to turn back," Sammi informed him solemnly. "HAPE at sixteen thousand."

"Is he all right?" Ethan asked in concern.

She shrugged. "He coughed a lot."

Ethan shook his head. "It makes you question Cap's judgment."

"Hey," Sammi said sharply. "You're talking about Cap Cicero. He stood on this summit and twenty others before we were even born."

"I *met* this kid," Ethan persisted. "Back in Kathmandu. He looks like he's in grade school."

"You've never climbed with him," she countered with more bravado than facts. "He's tough. He'll be back."

"That's what worries me," Ethan told her.

THE CLIMB

"You worry about your climb," Sammi suggested, "and we'll worry about ours. Right, Perry?"

"Right." Deep down, Perry knew he was worried enough for every expedition in Base Camp.

# CHAPTER SEVEN

http://www.summathletic.com/everest/
icefall

A mountain the size of Everest must be tackled in pieces and ascended slowly, traveling up to and then down from a series of camps. The first challenge is the perilous Khumbu Icefall, which stretches from Base Camp to Camp One at 19,500 feet.

If the glacier can be thought of as a frozen river moving at four feet per day, the Icefall is its Niagara. Here, it drops precipitously. But instead of a rush of cascading water, in the Icefall this means collapsing seracs — massive blocks of ice, some of them one hundred feet tall.

If the Icefall has become the most feared part of the route up Everest, it is also the most strikingly beautiful. **CLICK HERE** to see the SummitQuest climbers taking on the vertical minefield of the Khumbu Icefall.

The crevasse was thirty feet wide and so deep that no bottom was visible, only a steely blue-gray darkening to black. Sammi Moon balanced precariously on an aluminum ladder — one of four lashed together to span the gap.

She turned back to her teammates, her face wreathed in smiles. "This is the coolest thing I've ever done — and I've done a lot of cool things!"

Cicero rolled his eyes. "Sometime this year, please."

She scampered to the other side, and then it was Perry's turn. His crampons scraped against the first aluminum rung, and he froze.

"Hurry up," grumbled Tilt.

"Come on, Perry," Sammi encouraged, so close, yet so far away. "Don't look down."

But down was the only place to look. Tiptoeing across the metal rungs in cramponed boots was as tricky as it was terrifying. His first glimpse of the chasm's yawning maw nearly caused him to lose his breakfast.

*No,* he thought. *No, Uncle Joe, I can't do this. I've gone on your rock scrambles and climbed your crags, but I won't walk a tightrope over a bottomless pit!*

There was a low rumble, and the ladder began to vibrate. Suddenly, a quarter mile away, a huge section of the Icefall disintegrated with an earsplitting roar, sending seracs the size of houses tumbling like tenpins.

Perry was glued to the spot, waiting out the earthquake. Trembling along with the tremors.

Cicero himself had said it best three hours before as the team was strapping on crampons and harnesses in the predawn chill: "You're walking into the last great democracy in the world. The Icefall doesn't care if you're the best climber in the world or the worst. If you're unlucky up there, you're dead, and there's nothing anybody can do about it. So I guess the rule is: Don't be unlucky."

Not exactly reassuring words.

Perry lifted his left foot and placed it ahead of the right. It was a tiny step, but it brought him twelve inches closer to being done with this. Then came the right and another twelve inches. The others were cheering like this was a triumph, but Perry knew it was really a form of surrender — surrender to Uncle Joe, nine thousand miles away. As his crampons crunched the ice beside Sammi, it occurred to him that, on the other side of the world, Uncle Joe was probably asleep right now, unaware of his victory.

In a remarkable show of skill and courage, Sneezy lowered himself on a rope several feet down into the crevasse so he could film Tilt's

crossing from below. As he passed over the camera, Tilt looked down and mouthed the words, "Hi, Mom."

"Watch," he whispered to Sammi on the other side. "Twenty bucks says Baboon bends the ladder."

"Climbing with your mouth again, huh?" Sammi observed. "How do you keep your teeth from getting stuck in the glacier?"

"It has to bug you, too," Tilt persisted. "We break our necks getting in shape, and then Cap hires a waterbed to be our Sirdar." The Sirdar was the leader of the Sherpas.

At last, the six were reunited beyond the crevasse. Dr. Oberman and Dominic were not there. They remained in the valley, awaiting the boy's recovery from HAPE.

Passage through the Icefall was nerve-wracking and difficult, but at least the trail was set. Each year, two Sherpas were hired as "Icefall doctors." So the SummitQuest team was following an established route with fixed ropes and ladders.

Perry never got used to it. His one strength as a climber was his ropework. It was a product of his nervousness, really. He was always so afraid of falling that he had become an expert at securing himself with safety lines bolted or screwed into the mountain. But here on Everest, the ropes were all fixed, rendering his talent useless. In the Icefall, an alpinist relied not on technical skill, but on a mixture of courage, blind faith, and pure stubbornness that bordered on insanity. Every time he set foot on a ladder, the terror was so immediate that his abdomen ached from clenching his stomach. In his school chess club back home, he was renowned as the guy who wasn't afraid to take risks. *Risks!* he thought bitterly. No chess player ever knew the meaning of the word. *In chess, the worst that can happen is getting checkmated. Here, a bad risk can send you plummeting to an icy grave!*

Fatigue was also a major factor. They were climbing two thousand feet higher than Base Camp, and the air was thinning as they rose. Every few steps, Perry had to stop and gasp for breath. Although the temperature was barely above zero, he was bathed in perspiration. His one consolation was that Tilt, with the physique of a rhino and twice the strength, was also puffing and sweating. The grin was gone from Sammi's face, replaced by a grimace of effort. Even Himalayan legend Cap Cicero slowed a little. Only Babu, born and raised at altitude, waddled along with no loss of speed.

"You're right," Sammi panted sarcastically to Tilt. "He's going to collapse any minute."

THE CLIMB

"Shut up."

The percussive drumrolls caused by splintering ice never stopped for a second. It was a chilling reminder that anything — even the ground beneath your feet — could crumble at any moment.

They had been in the Icefall nearly six hours when the fixed ropes angled sharply upward. It was by no means the steepest part of the route, but this time they were climbing a single colossal serac. Shaped like a shark's tooth the size of the Statue of Liberty, it towered over them, lord of the Icefall, leaning ominously forward.

Cicero sucked air between his teeth. "I don't like the look of that."

For Perry, who hadn't liked the look of anything since Base Camp, the pronouncement was a 9-1-1 call to every nerve ending in his body. "We're turning around, right?" he babbled. "We'll head down and find the Icefall doctors, and they'll rework the route — "

"I'll go first," Sammi interrupted.

One by one, they ascended the shark's tooth. With every heart-stopping footfall, Perry tried to beam his terror and misery across continents and oceans to Joe Sullivan's safe, warm bed in Boulder, Colorado. *I hope you're having a nightmare, Uncle Joe!* he thought bitterly. *I'm having one in broad daylight.*

Forty-five minutes later, the six stood at Camp One — a ragtag assortment of tents that stood at the entrance to the Western Cwm, the highest canyon on the planet.

Cicero was pleased. "Nice work. A little slow, but that'll improve as we get used to the thin air." Then he dropped the bombshell. "Ten minutes break, and we go back down."

"Down?!" protested Tilt. "You mean we're not staying at Camp One?"

"We're not ready for this altitude. Climb high, sleep low — that's the rule." He chuckled. "Don't worry, the descent is the fun part. It isn't any easier, but it takes half the time."

*And double the stomach lining,* reflected Perry, who felt his guts churning again.

So they turned around and headed back into the Icefall.

It happened just as Sammi was clipping her harness onto the fixed line to descend the massive shark's tooth. All at once, there was a crack as loud as a gunshot, followed by a mournful groaning sound, and the 150-foot serac began to topple forward.

"Jump!" bellowed Cicero.

# CHAPTER EIGHT

Sammi leaped, swinging her legs up and clear, as the mountain of ice rolled over on its face, bringing with it the destructive power of a small nuclear bomb. The climbers below ran for cover as shattering ice flew every which way. The screw at the bottom anchoring the fixed rope snapped like a toothpick, and the line popped loose and hung there. With a cry of terror, Sammi plummeted 150 feet straight down, still harnessed to the useless rope.

In a spectacular display of speed for someone his size, Babu Pemba sprang into action. It was technically impossible to run in crampons, but he came close, hurling himself forward like an NFL linebacker making a highlight-film tackle.

He hit the ice a split second before Sammi hit him. He couldn't catch her — from that height, the impact would have crushed him. Instead, he redirected the free-falling climber to strike the glacier at an angle, and they rolled, somersaulting one over the other. They would have kept on going, tumbling and sliding until a crevasse swal-

EVEREST

lowed them, if they hadn't smacked into a glacial chunk the size of a small truck — a fragment of the former shark's tooth.

"*Sammi!*" With the route gone, Cicero was front-pointing down a 150-foot drop with a single ax. "*Babu!*"

"I'm okay!" called Sammi. Babu sat up beside her, and she clamped her arms around his hefty frame, mumbling, "At least I *think* I'm okay . . . I can't believe I'm okay."

Sneezy rushed up, Tilt and Perry hot on his heels. The guide set down the camera and examined Sammi and Babu inch by inch. Only then did he flash Cicero a thumbs-up.

"Thank God!" But the team leader didn't relax until he himself had made it down to stand with his Sirdar and his teenage charge.

"Take some time," he told Sammi. "As much as you need. I don't want you climbing again until you're one-hundred-percent comfortable."

"Are you kidding?" she scoffed. "You know me, Cap. I like it like that. Gets the blood pumping."

"That was almost prom night, your wedding — the rest of your life," he said seriously. "Be a strong, silent type if you like. But we're not moving until you admit what almost happened."

THE CLIMB

"Silly," she chided sweetly. "Sophomores don't go to prom."

But Cicero knew her bravado was just an act. Three hours later, when the exhausted team staggered back into Base Camp, Sammi Moon was still shaking.

The monotonous chanting seemed to float on the thin air as easily as the low overcast.

It was Dominic's second visit to the famous monastery at Thyangboche. Ten days before he had come eagerly to this rambling collection of temples, almost as much of a landmark on the mountaineering map as Everest itself.

Now the place merely reminded him of where he was not.

*Patience,* he told himself.

After five days at lower altitude, he had made a complete recovery from HAPE. It was astounding, Dr. Oberman assured him. Normally it took close to two weeks for the effects of altitude sickness to disappear.

He believed her. He could see it in her eyes as she poked and prodded him with her stethoscope. Yes, his chest was clear, although the dry Khumbu cough still plagued him. She kept raving about his healing power, but when he asked when they would start back up the valley, the answer was always the same.

"It's not time yet."

*Will it ever be time?*

"What does Cap say?" he would ask every night. "Did you talk to him?"

"Cap hired a doctor for his expedition. If he had medical training, he wouldn't need me."

He sat in the temple, with a *kata* — a white silk prayer scarf — draped around his neck. He was glumly sipping sweet tea when he spied an emaciated elderly lama. The man was so weak that he had to be carried in by several of his colleagues. All at once, the monk pointed at Dominic and began speaking in such agitation that he had to be restrained by his bearers.

Dominic and Dr. Oberman left soon after — they didn't want to be the cause of any disturbance. But as they made their way to the door, one of the younger lamas rushed up and addressed them in broken English. He apologized for the elderly monk frightening them. The man was coming off a three-week fast.

"But what was he saying about me?" asked Dominic

"He say, look this boy, he have shiny coils all around," the young lama informed him.

THE CLIMB

"Shiny coils?" repeated Dominic. "You mean like climbing ropes? They can look kind of shiny in bright sun."

The doctor shook her head. "It was just a hallucination."

The young monk was offended. "No hallucinate! *Vision!* Very important. Always remember."

"I — I will," Dominic managed as Dr. Oberman led him outside.

When they had reached their lodge in the nearby village, she turned to him. "Tomorrow," she said, "we'll start back up toward Base Camp. No guarantees, okay? We'll take it one day at a time."

Her cautious tone did nothing to dampen his celebration.

That night, he lay on his lumpy mattress, looking up at a small glass vial on a leather string. It held sand from the Dead Sea — the lowest point on Earth. The keepsake belonged to his brother, Chris, a gift from their grandmother before Dominic was even born. Chris had been planning to leave it on the summit of Everest. "From the bottom of the world to the top." That was his motto. And when Chris had been cut from the team, he had passed it on to Dominic.

*Hang on, Chris. We're still in this thing.*

Despite his exhilaration, he was strangely

troubled. The incident at the monastery was still very much on his mind.

Shiny coils. Did it mean ropes? Could the holy man actually have seen a vision of Dominic ascending the mountain?

*More likely it's a scam,* he thought. *They say it to every climber who goes in there.*

But there was another possible explanation for the shiny coils: Medical tubes and wires, snaking in and around his body.

In a hospital.

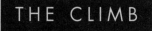

THE CLIMB

# CHAPTER NINE

SummitQuest's next foray onto the shanks of Everest was a climb to Camp One for a two-day acclimatization stay.

If boredom had been an annoyance at Base Camp, here at 19,500 feet it was a full-fledged epidemic. There was absolutely nothing to do except read and melt snow into drinking water.

Perry looked into the pot. "The fire's broken," he complained, stirring a mound of slush that seemed determined to stay slush forever.

Sneezy laughed. "Fire burns cooler at altitude. Wait till Camp Four. You can spend a whole night trying to make a cup of soup."

Tilt headed for the tent flap. "I'm not thirsty."

The cameraman grabbed him by the arm. "If you get dehydrated on Everest, you're dead. Make yourself comfortable. We're going to be here a long time."

In contrast to the chill of the Icefall, the Western Cwm was like a giant solar oven. They were sandwiched between the Nuptse wall and the west shoulder of Everest. The sun's rays baked

EVEREST

the snow valley, raising the temperature well into the nineties.

"This is bizarre," complained Sammi. "I'm going to fry on a sheet of ice."

Stripping off layers of clothing was the only way to stay comfortable. But this far up into the atmosphere, there was practically zero protection from the sun's rays. Unprotected skin burned in minutes. They slathered on sunscreen, but in less than an hour they were forced to flee to the unmoving hot air of the tents.

"It beats being broiled," said Perry.

"So much nicer to be slow-roasted," growled Tilt.

At that moment, Cicero burst in, brandishing his walkie-talkie like a club. "Base Camp just patched me through to the satellite phone so I could take a call from Summit headquarters back in the States. They're getting flak because maybe Dominic isn't up to this climb."

"But how could they know anything's wrong with Dominic?" asked Sammi.

"Because they read it in the *National Daily*, that's how!" roared Cicero.

There was silence as the meaning of his words sank in. During training camp in Colorado, there had been a tell-all story in the *Na-*

*tional Daily*, but everyone assumed that the source was a disgruntled climber who had been cut from the team. This latest leak could only have come from someone at Mount Everest.

Tilt held his breath and did his best not to panic. *There's no way Cap could know it's me*, he kept repeating to himself. *There's no way Cap could know it's me. . . .*

Sammi spoke up. "What about Ethan Zaph? He knows Dominic had HAPE."

"But Ethan wasn't in boot camp," Perry pointed out.

Tilt came alive. "Maybe not in person," he argued, "but he had a lot of friends in that group. We were the top young climbers in the country. If he wanted info, he just had to pick up the phone."

"He could have said, 'Hi, it's Z-man. What's new at boot camp?'" Sammi agreed. "No one would suspect he was fishing."

Cicero was skeptical. "Why should Zaph care if Dominic gets a shot at Everest?"

"It's *his* record we're out to break," Tilt explained, thrilled to have a theory that deflected suspicion from himself. "Any trouble he can make for SummitQuest could affect our chances of getting to the top."

Cicero thought it over. "Maybe," he said finally. "But whoever it is, the walls have ears, so keep your mouths shut, especially around Zaph. Got it?"

Tilt cleared his throat. "Have you heard anything from Dominic? Is he getting better? You know, better enough to climb with us?"

"*I* decide whether Dominic climbs or not!" Cicero snapped testily. "Not the *National Daily* and whatever bigmouth is feeding them their information. And if I find out that it's one of you, I don't care if you're three steps from the summit — so help me, I'll yank you down to Base Camp myself and put you on the next yak to Kathmandu. Is that clear?"

Tilt nodded along with the others, his stomach tight.

Sammi wasn't the only one who lived on the edge.

By the time Dr. Oberman and Dominic made it to Base Camp, the SummitQuest team had returned from Camp One, rested, and set out again.

"How do you feel, kid?" asked Cicero over the walkie-talkie from Camp Two, nearly a mile above.

"Fantastic," Dominic told him. Tackling the

THE CLIMB

trek at a snail's pace had been frustrating, but his strength had returned in full force. "We can come up and meet you guys if you want."

"Cool your jets," laughed Cicero. "Get used to the altitude at Base Camp. We'll be back in a few days."

But even Base Camp — a place Dominic had been dreaming about for half his life — couldn't hold his interest for very long.

"Andrea," he suggested the next morning, "why don't we suit up and go into the Icefall?"

"You heard Cap," she told him. "We wait here for the rest of the group."

"We don't even have to make it to Camp One," he wheedled. "Come on, let's get our feet wet. I haven't strapped on crampons in six weeks."

"Dominic, you know better than anybody the dangers of going too high too fast. Do you have any idea how lucky you are? Not only are you alive, but you're probably going to get your chance at the mountain. Be grateful."

Dominic was nervous. The others were on their third acclimatization trip, and he hadn't even started yet. There were still weeks to go before they could try for the peak, but a lot could go wrong on Mount Everest. A few days of bad weather could put him so far behind schedule that he'd never be ready for a summit bid.

Stuck in a tent at Base Camp while the rest of them push for the top. Nothing, he thought, not even HAPE, could be worse than that!

The next morning, there was an accident on the Lhotse Face. One of the Japanese climbers was struck in the head by a falling rock.

A group of Sherpas were attempting a rescue. They had the man strapped to a ladder and were slowly carrying him down through the Icefall. This was nothing short of heroism — the Icefall was difficult and dangerous enough without having to maneuver a 180-pound climber attached to an eight-foot length of aluminum. As the only doctor presently in Base Camp, Andrea Oberman rushed the quarter mile to the mouth of the Icefall to await the patient. Dominic went with her.

Half an hour later, the party appeared. The rescuers were led by none other than Babu, supporting the front of the ladder/stretcher on his shoulders.

"What can I do to help?" Dominic asked Dr. Oberman.

The doctor had no time for him. "Stand clear, Dominic. This man may have a fractured skull."

She turned to Babu. "Get on the radio and set up a helicopter evacuation!" The barked orders continued to the group in general. "Let's move h▓ back to camp! Bring extra blankets! Where's ▓ best place to land a chopper around here?"

The Japanese mountaineer was carried off. Dominic made a move to follow, but hesitated. There were plenty of volunteers for this rescue. He'd only get in the way.

He peered up into the shattered glacier.

So dangerous. Why was he drawn to it?

The answer came immediately: *I'm a climber.*

"You're all crazy," his mother had said years before, when Mr. Alexis had decided to spend Thanksgiving scaling Half Dome in Yosemite. Chris had been only twelve for that trip — one of the youngest ever to take on the famous wall. Nine-and-a-half-year-old Dominic had burned with jealousy. It had always been that way — Chris was older; Chris was bigger; Chris was better. Even at training camp for SummitQuest, Chris had been considered a sure thing; Dominic had been expected to disappear in the first cut.

Yet Dominic, not Chris, was the Alexis brother standing at the entrance to the Khumbu Icefall. Dominic was at the base of mighty Everest.

And what was he doing?

Waiting.

That was when his eyes fell on the assortment of equipment lying on the moraine ten yards away. Since it was so difficult to walk in crampons over the Base Camp rocks, most Everesters left their footgear by the entrance to the Icefall. Camp, after all, was still a quarter mile away. For an exhausted, dehydrated climber returning from the upper mountain, it was a way to save precious energy.

Dominic's crampons were easy to find — they were the smallest ones there by at least three sizes. His ice ax, also smaller, lay beside them. He hefted it experimentally.

*You promised Cap you'd stay put,* he reminded himself.

But every time he turned the thought over in his head, it lost a little more shine, fading next to a new notion, growing in intensity.

*I'll only go in for an hour or so. Just to get the feel of it.*

# CHAPTER TEN

To Dominic, the Khumbu Icefall was the most beautiful place on Earth.

Of course he knew his surroundings could be lethal. Climbers in the Icefall were like ants on a bowling ball — the slightest movement could crush you with a force millions of times your own weight. Even the greatest alpinists in history — Cap Cicero included — had a healthy fear of the Icefall. Dominic climbed cautiously, with a humble respect for the hazards all around. But he could not bring himself to be afraid. Instead, he was filled with wonderment at this vertical labyrinth of deep blue crystal. Every ray of sunlight that managed to squeeze down between Everest and Nuptse was multiplied to infinity by a wonderland of irregular prisms.

When he came to the first ladder, disappointment washed over him. That was the deal he'd made with himself. He would ascend only as far as the Icefall's first crevasse. Then it would be time to turn around. He was not dressed properly — sweats and a jacket instead of the standard one-piece wind suit. He had found light gloves in

EVEREST

the pockets, but not the Gore-Tex mitts for high-altitude mountaineering.

He frowned. On the other hand, the Icefall was rarely windy, and the day was just beginning to warm. He'd only been climbing for forty minutes. It didn't make sense to come this far without crossing one of the Khumbu's notorious ladders.

*Over and back — that's all. Just so I'll know what to expect.*

His crampons scraped at the rungs of the ladder. Awkward steps. His eyes began to fill with tears. Not tears of terror, but the emotion of feeling eighty years of mountaineering history under his feet. This wasn't a drill, or a practice climb designed to *simulate* Everest. This was the real thing.

A sudden voice behind him interrupted his reverie.

"Just walk, sahib. No look down hole. Pretend not there."

Startled, Dominic craned his neck to glance over his shoulder. At the foot of the ladder stood three Sherpas carrying enormous loads.

The leader stared at him. "A child?"

"I'm with SummitQuest," Dominic called back a little defensively. "Cap Cicero's team." He hurried across the ladder.

One by one, the Sherpas followed, joining him on the other side of the crevasse. They were barely breathing hard despite the huge packs each man carried. Sherpas were employed to ferry gear and supplies to the high camps on the mountain. They received little credit for their efforts, but without them, no expedition would have a chance at the summit.

The Sirdar looked him up and down. "You very young." Unlike Babu, who had lived in the West, most Sherpas spoke broken English with thick accents.

Dominic nodded. "We're all kids on SummitQuest," he admitted, "but I'm the youngest."

"You stay with us," the Sirdar decided. "No climb alone. Icefall dangerous."

*But I was just about to go back down —*

Dominic opened his mouth to say it, but bit his lip instead. How could he pass up a chance to climb with Sherpas, the legendary unsung heroes of Everest? *Just a little farther,* he decided. *Then I'll turn around.* After all, the descent would be much quicker. Andrea had her hands full with the injured Japanese climber. Dominic would be back in Base Camp before she even missed him.

He climbed a while longer, marveling at the porters' ease despite their backbreaking burdens.

Then it happened. On a steep, tricky scramble, there was a sudden snap. A crampon tumbled down the rime, its broken strap trailing behind it. The climbers stood frozen as it skittered out of reach and disappeared into the space between two blocks of ice.

The tallest Sherpa dropped his pack and onefooted it down the slope in search of his gear. Negotiating the Icefall was difficult enough under the best of circumstances. Without crampons, it was practically suicidal.

The man peered into the gap, then looked up with a gesture of helplessness that was clear in any language. The crampon was gone for good.

For Dominic, it was a sobering reminder: Yes, Everest was climbable. But let the slightest thing go wrong — something as simple as a broken strap — and all bets were off.

The Sherpas held a worried conference. Pasang could not continue his carry to Camp One. He would be able to make it back to Base Camp on one crampon, but that meant his load would have to sit in the Icefall until one of the others could come back for it.

As they debated all of their options, Dominic shrugged into the heavy shoulder harness and lifted Pasang's pack. "I'll take it."

The Sirdar stared at him. "Too heavy for boy."

"I can manage," Dominic assured them.

THE CLIMB

But the Sherpas insisted on transferring some of Dominic's load to their own. By the time Pasang left them and the climb resumed, Dominic guessed that his pack held twenty-five or thirty pounds of equipment.

It occurred to him that this might be unwise — to carry a load to nearly twenty thousand feet so soon after his bout with HAPE. But the truth was he felt remarkably strong. Most climbers wound up gasping for breath on their first trip through the Icefall. And sure, he found the air thin, but it didn't seem to be slowing him down.

Maybe Dr. Oberman was right. His extra week along the trekking route had trained his blood to carry more oxygen to the brain. He was *acclimatized*!

The gear turned out to be headed for the This Way Up expedition. Awaiting it at Camp One was none other than Ethan Zaph.

The youngest summiteer in Everest history did a double take when he saw Dominic unloading his pack. "What are *you* doing here? You went home! You had HAPE!"

Dominic shrugged. "I got better."

And he turned to follow his Sherpa team back into the Icefall for the descent, leaving Ethan standing there with his jaw dropped.

They were down in a little over two hours.

Pasang met them on the moraine, carrying steaming cups of Sherpa tea. There was one for Dominic as well. In all his life, nothing had ever tasted sweeter.

There was other good news besides Pasang's safe return on only one crampon. The injured Japanese climber had been safely evacuated by helicopter and was expected to recover.

"Congratulations," Dominic told Dr. Oberman when he joined her at the SummitQuest camp. "I hear the guy's going to be okay."

"Thanks." She looked him up and down. "You're all sweaty. What have you been up to?"

*Oh, about 19,500 feet,* he thought with a grin. Aloud, he said, "I helped out some Sherpas."

He didn't mention that this had been the greatest day of his life. Or that his mind was now occupied with a single thought: *I've got to get back up there!*

THE CLIMB

# CHAPTER ELEVEN

http://www.summathletic.com/everest/
cwm

The Western Cwm, the highest canyon on the planet, is located between the Nuptse wall and the West Shoulder of Everest. It has been nicknamed the "Crevasse Highway." Here, the Khumbu glacier splits into hundreds of pieces, separated by crevasses measuring as much as eighty feet across.

Camp Two, at 21,300 feet, is also known as Advance Base Camp, or ABC. Unlike the tiny Camp One, it is a bustling community of more than one hundred tents and the main destination for acclimatization. Climbers can and do spend as long as a week at a time here, adjusting their bodies to the thin air they'll encounter higher on the mountain. At ABC, the biggest enemy is not the altitude, the extreme heat of day or cold of night, or even the yawning crevasses.

EVEREST

**CLICK HERE** to see members of SummitQuest grappling with the mind-numbing boredom of Camp Two, where nothing ever happens.

Perry was chipping ice to melt for drinking water when he saw the creature. It was about nine feet tall and walked upright, its light brown fur standing out against the terraced ice of the West Shoulder — seventy yards away and closing fast!

He was about to yell for Cicero when there was a terrific commotion in the This Way Up camp. The half-demented voice of Nestor Ali rang out, "Get your camera! It's a yeti! A *real* one!"

He burst out of his tent lens first, shooting pictures at the speed of light.

That was when Perry noticed that the "yeti" was wearing crampons. The mythical abominable snowman beat its chest and came running toward Nestor. The climber/journalist dropped his camera in the snow and took off running, with no crampons, wearing only his soft-soled boot liners. He was soon flat on his back on the hard-packed snow.

The yeti advanced menacingly on him. Then,

THE CLIMB

only a few feet away from the kill, the giant creature split in half. The top hit the rime and rolled
away, giggling. The bottom was Ethan Zaph.

By this time, a large crowd of climbers had
gathered to watch as Nestor scrambled to his
feet.

"Very funny, guys! Very funny!" he ranted, his
boot liners slipping. "I bet you'd be laughing
your heads off if I'd run straight into a crevasse!"

Ethan was in hysterics. "We got you, Nestor!
We've been carrying this fur coat for weeks!
*Weeks!* Ever since Namche!" He picked up the
coat to reveal the top half of the Yeti, the Sherpa
Pasang.

For a group of bored-stiff climbers at Camp
Two, these events were the equivalent of Acad-
emy Award entertainment. Raucous laughter and
wild cheering rocked the Cwm. Even seasoned
veterans like Cicero guffawed their approval at
this distraction from the serious business of climbing a behemoth.

At last, even Nestor good-naturedly joined the
party. "Okay," he said, "but if my camera's broken — "

A low rumbling in the Cwm rose above the
merriment.

Babu was the first to stop chuckling, followed

by Cicero, who called for silence. There was an explosion like a kiloton of dynamite, and the snow pack on the West Shoulder disintegrated and began to roar down at them.

*"Run!"* bellowed Cicero.

No instruction was ever less necessary. There was a mass stampede for the Nuptse side of the valley. Perry stumbled, but Sneezy hauled him up by a fistful of sweatshirt and dragged him out of harm's way.

The avalanche thundered down to the Cwm, kicking up a cloud of ice crystals that rose hundreds of feet in the air. The churning wall of snow pounced on Camp Two, shattering the outer ring of tents and leaving the others half buried.

Then, all at once, it was over. The silence of the Cwm belied the furious activity of the previous moments.

The head counts began. The various expeditions took inventory of their snow-covered personnel and reported no one missing. Except —

"Wait a minute!" Cicero's voice rang out. "Where's Moon?"

Desperately, Babu, Sneezy, Tilt, and Perry searched faces. Sammi was nowhere to be found.

*"Sammi!"* Cicero raced for the compound,

wading through thigh-high powder. Using his hands as a shovel, he dug out the tent flap and zipped it open.

There sat Sammi Moon, cross-legged on her air mattress, completely lost in the musical world of her Walkman. Through the pummeling beat and raging guitars of Green Day, she had simply not noticed the avalanche.

Weak with relief, Cicero reached out and snatched the headphones from her ears. "Hey," he said hoarsely, "ever consider turning down the volume on that thing?"

"Thanks, Dad," Sammi grinned. She looked up at him and stared. The team leader was frosted white from head to toe. "Man, that must have been some snowball fight. I miss all the good stuff."

# CHAPTER TWELVE

Climbers and Sherpas alike set about the task of digging out the tents. In a few hours, Advance Base Camp was up and running again.

Although no one had been injured, four campsites had been destroyed. One of these belonged to This Way Up. So Ethan, Nestor, and their teammates and Sherpas headed back down toward the Icefall. With Ethan's departure came a release of tension in the SummitQuest group. Most of them suspected Ethan of leaking information about them to the *National Daily*. Only Tilt knew the truth.

Porters continued to plod up the Cwm, carrying loads destined for Camp Three on the Lhotse Face and Camp Four on the South Col. ABC was the obvious rest stop, and it was not uncommon to see as many as thirty Sherpas sitting on the snowpack, eating candy bars and drinking tea.

Cicero and Sneezy were huddled over the video camera, examining the day's footage. The images they chose would be E-mailed by satellite phone directly from Camp Two to Summit's Web site designers in Colorado. Scenes from the expedition could be on-line in a matter of hours.

Babu tapped Cicero on the shoulder. "Got a minute?"

"What's up?"

"I've been hearing the Sherpas talking about someone they call the 'little sahib.' The word is there's this kid — just a boy — who's been helping them carry loads through the Icefall for the last couple of days."

Cicero's face flamed red. "I'll kill him!"

"That's impossible!" exclaimed Sneezy. "How could it be Dominic? The kid was in a Gamow bag a week ago."

"Then who is it?" snarled Cicero. "One of the dozens of other thirteen-year-olds hanging around Mount Everest?"

"For what it's worth," added Babu, "they say he climbs like one of us."

Cicero reached for the radio and hailed Base Camp. A moment later, Dr. Oberman answered his call.

"This is Andrea."

"Where's Dominic?" Cicero practically barked at her.

"He's around somewhere," came the reply. "You know Dominic; he marches to the beat of a different drummer. He's made friends with some of the Sherpas, and they honestly seem to love him."

"Of course they love him!" howled Cicero. "He's been doing their work for them!"

"What work?"

"He's carrying loads up the Icefall!"

There was a pause, then the doctor's voice said quietly but clearly, "I'll kill him."

"Get in line!" growled Cicero. "Listen, if you find him, sit on him. I'm coming down." He began to strap on his crampons.

Babu reached for his own gear.

"God, no!" Cicero exclaimed. "I need you here to keep an eye on these three so they don't start a summit push without us!" He shouldered a small pack. "What happened to us, Babu? We've been guiding this peak forever. How did we lose control?"

Babu shrugged. "We've got a good system that works on this mountain, but it's based on everybody being adults. If you tell a forty-year-old lawyer, 'Stay out of the Icefall,' and he doesn't, that's *his* problem. But if the same happens with a thirteen-year-old kid, you feel like it's your fault and you've let him down. We're climbers, Cap, not baby-sitters."

As Cicero began to descend the Cwm from Camp Two, his mind was in turmoil. Dominic. It was always Dominic. Cicero had known in boot camp that the kid was too young and too small. But the boy's surprising skill and indomitable spirit had won him over.

*And what's my reward for having faith in him?*

Who got HAPE on the trek? Who turned into the *National Daily*'s poster boy for "Send This Baby Home"? Summit headquarters had even begun to receive inquiries from the Nepalese authorities about why such a young child was listed on their climbing permit.

And now the little brat wouldn't stay out of the Icefall.

So lost was he in his internal rant that he barely even looked at the line of porters passing him in the other direction. They were Sherpas, climbing under heavy packs and making it look easy. He was almost past them when, with his peripheral vision, he noticed that one of them — the smallest — was wearing a SummitQuest hat.

"Freeze!"

Dominic looked up, surprised. "Oh, hi, Cap."

Cicero went to top volume. "You were sick, mister! Do you have any idea how *stupid* this is? And carrying all that weight makes it twice as likely that you'll have a relapse of HAPE!"

Dominic shrugged, load and all. "I feel really good."

Cicero stared at the boy. He *looked* really good, too. Cicero had guided enough expeditions to recognize a climber in difficulty. Dominic was rosy-cheeked and breathing well. He moved with a spring in his step despite a pack that must have weighed forty pounds.

But that didn't excuse the disobedience. "When I say stay in Base Camp, what code word is in there that tells you to start climbing? And now you're in the Cwm, so I guess the Icefall isn't good enough for you anymore! Where were you planning to stop? The summit? Or were you going to continue on to the moon?"

Dominic looked stricken. "I'm sorry, Cap. It just sort of got away from me."

Cicero was not receptive to his argument. "Too much candy on Halloween Night — *that* gets away from you! Not the Icefall! Climbing through the most inhospitable landscape on the planet is something you do on *purpose!* Give me one good reason why I shouldn't pack you off to Kathmandu right now."

"I'll go down, Cap. I promise. I just have to deliver this load to the Japanese camp at ABC."

Cicero swallowed his exasperation. That was

THE CLIMB

classic Dominic. Even when he was in big trouble, he wouldn't duck out on his responsibilities to a bunch of Japanese climbers he had never met.

"Give me that." The team leader yanked the pack off Dominic's back and hefted it himself. "You can sleep at Camp Two tonight and descend with the whole group tomorrow." A grunt of effort escaped him. "You carried this?"

The Sherpas laughed.

"Little sahib strong like yak," their Sirdar assured him. "For him, air no thin. Thick like sea level."

Cicero turned his face away to hide a smile of pride.

*Welcome back, kid.*

# CHAPTER THIRTEEN

Base Camp was at full capacity, a bustling town of five hundred inhabitants, not including the porters and yak trains that arrived several times each day. Expeditions were constantly heading in and out of the Icefall. Teams pushed to higher and higher camps to complete their final acclimatization trips. SummitQuest bounced back and forth between base and ABC, venturing as far as the bergschrund, the deep crevasse that separated the Western Cwm from the Lhotse Face. It was late April, and soon the weather windows would start opening. When that happened — when conditions on the upper mountain cleared for a brief period — everyone had to be ready. Most of the time, the Everest summit was battered by jet-stream winds so strong that they could be heard in Base Camp, more than two vertical miles below. The sound was like the roar of a freight train.

Dominic had been banned from carrying loads through the Icefall, but he still spent a lot of his spare time with his newfound Sherpa friends. Pasang was even introducing him to the lan-

THE CLIMB

guage. In return, Dominic was trying to teach him the words to "I've Been Working on the Railroad," the only English recording in Pasang's tiny home village.

The young man found the vocabulary very difficult. "What it means — *fiddly-eye-oh*?"

Dominic's Sherpa connections also provided him with every single piece of gossip in Base Camp. The Sherpas had the lowdown on everybody. Dominic knew who had the best summit chances (This Way Up) and the worst (the Guamanian brothers). Adventure Consultants had the best food, the Israelis had the best computer games, and the Canadians were the most polite. The strongest climber on the mountain that year was Babu Pemba, who turned out to be a kind of local hero. They also had a lot of respect for Cap Cicero and Ethan Zaph.

Sammi Moon turned out to be quite famous among the Sherpas because she was involved in every softball game, every Frisbee catch, and every arm-wrestling match at Base Camp. By contrast, no one had noticed Perry at all. If the reluctant climber hadn't had such striking red hair, he might have been totally invisible.

Tilt, however, had a reputation all his own. He had discovered that the yak drivers were so poor that they would do practically anything to earn a few extra rupees — mere pennies in U.S. money. So he kept a staff of personal servants to perform such tasks as rewinding his videotapes, tying his bootlaces, and recharging his laptop computer. The climbing Sherpas hated him for it.

"Sherpas poor, yes," said Pasang angrily, "but no slaves."

For his own part, Dominic was disgusted and embarrassed to be part of the same team as Tilt Crowley.

"Why can't he rewind his own videotapes?" he muttered to Pasang. "He spends all day cooped up in that tent. What else does he have to do?"

**E-mail Message**
**TO: bv@national-daily.com**
**SUBJECT: Dominic's return**

**Cap has brought that poor sick kid back to Base Camp. They don't care about Dominic. They just want the glory of putting a thirteen-year-old on the summit.**

That lousy Dominic! Every time Tilt thought about it, he wanted to break something. Dominic couldn't stay sick like everybody else with HAPE.

**THE CLIMB**

He had to come roaring back, carrying loads up the Icefall with the baboons.

*And Cicero thinks the sun shines out of his little shrimp butt!*

The thought made Tilt smolder. *If I went into the Icefall without permission, I'd be on a plane home tomorrow.*

It wasn't fair. Dominic got HAPE, and it actually *helped* him acclimatize. He was dancing around the Cwm while the rest of them were hammered by the altitude.

Not that the little runt was going to summit. But his chances had to be improved because he could breathe the thin air.

*There must be some way to turn this around!*

**The really crazy part is that the Sherpas are taking advantage of Dominic, forcing him to haul heavy loads up through the Icefall. And Cap is doing nothing to stop it. Back in the States, you could go to jail for something like that, couldn't you? But in this dump, nobody cares.**

*There,* he thought with a grim smile. *That ought to keep the pot boiling.* By this time, Tilt had learned to anticipate the chain of events: The story comes out in the *National Daily*; outraged people complain to Summit; Summit chews out Cap Cicero.

And, he reflected with satisfaction, Cicero blames the whole thing on Ethan Zaph.

If Ethan was not too popular around the Summit-Quest campsite, his teammate, Nestor Ali, was becoming a great favorite. Young, and even younger at heart, Nestor was easygoing, friendly, and always good for a laugh. The yeti incident at ABC had only cemented his reputation as Everest clown. He was welcome in every tent and could often be found sitting around the flat stone slab that served as SummitQuest's dinner table.

"I don't think Ethan could be doing what you think he's doing," Nestor was saying one day over an omelet lunch. "Sure, he has the media contacts — he's a famous guy. But he doesn't care about records and being a big shot. He's a tunnel-vision climber. When he's taking aim at the summit, he forgets the rest of us are even here."

"Don't you think we're all like that?" Dominic asked thoughtfully. "I know I'm totally focused on getting my brother's sand to the top."

Nestor looked bewildered. "You're going to put *sand* on the summit? Why? To make sure nobody slips off?"

Dominic laughed. "Chris has sand from the Dead Sea," he explained, flipping up the leather string so the vial showed above his collar. "You know — from the bottom of the world to the top. Like that. If I get to the summit, I'll leave it up there for Chris. He should really be here, not me."

"I promised Caleb I'd take him to the top," Sammi said sheepishly. "I've got a picture of the two of us skydiving last summer — free fall."

"My uncle gave me an old piton from his rock-climbing days," Perry ventured. "He says it saved his life when he was twenty."

"Pretty lame for a billionaire," put in Tilt. "You'd think he'd give you the Hope diamond or something."

"This cost almost as much," Perry chuckled wanly. "It had to be pulled out of a cliff in the Canadian Rockies. It took a five-man team to find it and get it down."

"What about you, Nestor?" prompted Sammi. "Got anything for the pinnacle of the world?"

"My Slinky," Nestor replied readily.

"Slinky?" Perry repeated. "Like the kids' toy? Why would you want to leave *that* on the summit?"

"The ads say those things can 'walk' down any sloped surface," Nestor explained. "Well, if that's true, I can start it going at the top and it should boing all the way down the Kangshung face eleven thousand feet into Tibet."

There were howls of laughter from everyone but Tilt.

"You guys are nuts," he snorted.

"Well, what are *you* taking to the summit?" Sammi challenged.

Tilt kicked back on the air mattress. "Myself," he boasted. "And a camera to prove I got there."

# CHAPTER FOURTEEN

www.summathletic.com/everest/
lhotseface

Above the Western Cwm looms the mile-high wall of ice known as the Lhotse Face. It is the steepest part of the southeast ridge route and grows steeper as the climber ascends.

__CLICK HERE__ to see the SummitQuest team front-pointing up the sixty-degree slope, watched over by the spectacular peak of Lhotse, the fourth highest mountain in the world.

*Lhotse, my butt!* Perry thought to himself. He couldn't see any peak, spectacular or otherwise, towering above them. His universe at that moment consisted of a single rope that angled nearly straight up until it disappeared into a snow squall. For all he could tell, the upper end was attached to the Goodyear blimp.

He knew Lhotse was there only because the

rocks that kept pelting down had to be coming from somewhere. It was like climbing in a shooting gallery. And if one of them ever hit him . . .

He was clipped to the nylon line by means of a jumar, a device that enabled him to ascend the rope, but would lock automatically if he happened to fall.

*Slide jumar up six inches. Left foot. Right foot. Repeat fifty million times.*

The slope was too steep for conventional walking, yet not quite vertical enough for frontpointing. He found himself trying to do both — flat steps and toe steps — an awkward, ankletwisting combination more common on a ballet stage than in the Himalayas.

*But no ballet dancer could handle twenty-three thousand feet!*

"Doing fine, Noonan," called Cicero from below.

But Perry was not doing fine. The altitude was showing itself as a jackhammer against every single muscle he tried to move. The air was so thin that there was literally nothing to breathe. Every few feet he had to stop to rest, to take several more gasping sucks at the punishing atmosphere in the hope of inhaling a decent amount of oxygen so he could keep going.

The radiant heat of the Western Cwm may as

well have happened in another life. The Lhotse Face was capital-C Cold. His climber's watch registered it as twelve below zero. But that didn't account for the chill factor from a brutalizing wind.

Three hours of pure agony seemed to bring him closer to nowhere. On top of all its other miseries, the Lhotse Face was endless. Sneezy had put it best at Camp Two last night: "There's lotsa face up there!"

At 23,700 feet, they encountered two members of the Japanese team descending after a night at Camp Three. Perry had been dreading this. Since there was only a single fixed rope, climbers could not pass each other without one of them unhooking from the line. It would only be for a second or two, but at that moment, he or she would be connected to the mountain by nothing more than crampons.

And then the maneuver was upon him. The first man unhooked and stepped deftly around Perry. His partner seemed to be having a much harder time. He came down to Perry's level and just hung there, waiting. He was gasping as if he'd just run a marathon; his arms hung limp at his sides. There wasn't an ounce of extra energy in him.

Perry really had no choice. With a silent

prayer, he disconnected his jumar and moved to step around the other climber. Just as Perry was about to clip on again, the exhausted man somehow lost traction in his crampons and began to slide down the ice. His rope caught Perry just below the knees, dislodging both of the boy's front points from the Lhotse Face.

For an instant of exquisite terror, Perry Noonan was off that mountain. Then, all in the space of a split second, his jumar snapped into place, and the device's teeth bit into the rope, stopping a fall that had never really started.

He dangled there, motionless and palpitating, until his mind came back to him. Kicking both front points, he dropped to the face and hugged it as if he were trying to insert himself inside the ice.

"I'm alive," he mumbled. "I'm alive . . ."

He was still repeating those words an hour later when he finally arrived at Camp Three. The feeling of being untethered from the mountain, waiting for gravity to pitch him into the abyss, was with him for a very long time.

At twenty-four thousand feet, Camp Three was a place unfit for human habitation. For starters, there was no real camp — not in the sense of a

THE CLIMB

common area where people could sit and talk comfortably. Four two-person tents were perched precariously on ice that was pitched steeper than a log flume.

"Are you sure you made it small enough?" Tilt grumbled at Babu.

The Sirdar laughed. "Do you know how long it took four of us to hack out platforms flat enough for these tents? Nine hours. If you don't like it, try the Hilton."

They held a team powwow, nearly five miles above sea level across a slanted conference table of blue ice. The only way to do this was for the eight climbers to lie in the tents with their heads poking out the flaps, facing each other.

"I know exactly how you guys feel," said Cicero. "You can barely breathe; you've got pounding headaches; and energy-wise, if you had to scratch your noses, you wouldn't have the energy to raise your fingers that high. Now listen carefully, because I'm going to blow your minds: You're ready."

They looked at him dumbly.

"You are. We sleep here tonight, down to ABC tomorrow, and then back to Base Camp. Then we rest up and wait for good weather. And our next stop" — he rolled over and pointed straight up — "is *there*."

All eyes followed along. The overcast was beginning to break up and, a vertical mile above, the pinnacle of Everest peeked out from behind the bulk of the southwest face. The powerful jet-stream winds blew a plume of ice crystals off the summit half a mile into the troposphere.

# CHAPTER FIFTEEN

Tilt Crowley was watching *The Matrix* for the eighth time in the kitchen tent at Base Camp. Absently, he popped open his lunch, a single serving tin of tuna.

"Ugh!"

The tuna can was filled with sardines again! The merchants of Namche Bazaar were a bunch of crooks. They charged the expeditions top dollar and sold them mislabeled cat food. The word around Base Camp was that the French expedition had dropped a fortune on two cases of caviar and ended up with forty-eight single servings of refried beans.

*Maybe I'll get rich enough to buy Mount Everest and kick all the Sherpas out!*

"Cap! Cap!" It was Sammi's voice, obviously in a state of high excitement. A second later, she came bursting through the flap, Perry at her heels. "Where's Cap?"

"Don't know, don't care," yawned Tilt, pitching his tin of sardines through the opening out to the moraine.

EVEREST

"Some Nepal government guys just heli-coptered into camp!" Perry panted. "They're nos-ing around, asking questions about Dominic!"

Tilt was instantly alert. "What did you tell them?"

"What do you think I told them?" Sammi snapped. "I said, 'Dominic who?' If these two were sent because of the *National Daily*, they could be here to kick Dominic off the mountain!"

Tilt leaped to his feet. "Where's the shrimp now?"

They found Dominic in the This Way Up mess tent, drinking tea with Nestor, Pasang, and Gombu, the team's Base Camp Sirdar.

Sammi filled him in on the developments. "You've got to hide!" she finished.

"Oh, come on," scoffed Tilt. "What can they do to him? He's on the climbing permit. He's le-gal."

"That's not the problem," argued Nestor. "The government here can drive you crazy, even if you're legit. They'll delay you for weeks, crawl-ing all over you with a microscope. By the time you get the okay, the monsoon will roll in, and it'll be too late in the season to climb."

Dominic thought it over. "I'll disappear for a while."

THE CLIMB

"Whatever you do, do it fast," urged Perry, peering out the flap. "They just left our tent, and they're headed this way."

Gombu flipped open the expedition's pantry chest and began removing boxes of crackers, cookies, and cereal by the armload. "You safe in here!" he exclaimed, pushing Dominic inside. The others helped pile the light boxes on top of the fugitive.

"You don't have to bury him!" Tilt exploded. "Nobody's going to look in there anyway."

That was exactly the problem, Tilt thought to himself. The government guys weren't going to find Dominic unless Tilt ratted him out.

*But how can I do that in front of Sammi and Perry?*

"Shut the lid!" hissed Nestor. "They're almost here!"

And then the two officials were upon them. They wore olive green paramilitary uniforms and black berets. One of them held a murky faxed photograph of Dominic, an old school picture reproduced from one of the articles in the *National Daily*.

"We seek this boy," the leader said.

"He's not here," Nestor replied.

The two spoke to the Sherpas in Nepalese, and got very short answers and very long shrugs.

Tilt had the panicky feeling that they were about to leave. Both men were breathing hard — Base Camp was at high altitude, even for the people of Nepal. *Search the box.* He tried to send the message telepathically. *He's in the pantry chest.* But why would they ransack any one tent before looking in the over three hundred others first?

He decided that the Nepalese needed a little help. Perched on a camp stove were four aluminum nesting pots. He could "accidentally" hipcheck the cookware, which would clatter onto the pantry chest. With any luck, Dominic would be startled and cry out, thereby giving himself away.

"I have to go to the bathroom," Tilt mumbled and started forward. He was just angling into position, was about to deliver the blow, when —

"Who's talking to my people without me?"

Cicero burst through the flap, angry and arrogant as only a legend can afford to be. Tilt had no choice but to retreat as his team leader confronted the officials.

The constable with the fax stepped forward. "Cap Cicero, this is your climber, no?"

As he reached for the picture, Cicero intercepted a beseeching look from Sammi and noted that Perry's freckles were standing out like polka dots, so white was his face.

THE CLIMB

"Right," said Cicero. "Dominic Alexis."

"Where is he, please?"

Cicero never even paused. "Down in the valley somewhere. He's not going to climb. Too young, too small."

"A wise choice," the other man approved. "This news will be welcome at headquarters."

Perhaps closer to the truth, the news was welcomed by the two constables. They looked pathetically grateful to be able to head for their helicopter, which would take them away from 17,600 feet.

Ethan Zaph ducked in through the tent flap, peering quizzically over his shoulder. "What were those two guys doing here?"

Sammi fairly exploded in his face. "Like you don't know, rat!"

Cicero put a hand on her shoulder. "Take it easy, Moon."

Sammi was in no mood to be soothed. "Those two were looking to grab Dominic and kick him off the mountain!" she seethed at Ethan. "Because you've been feeding the *National Daily* lies about SummitQuest!"

Ethan stared at her, thunderstruck. Then he turned to Cicero. "What's she talking about, Cap? I know you guys don't like me because I quit your team. But why would you think I'd stab another climber in the back?"

"We don't know what to think, kid," said Cicero. "We're grappling with a lot of things ourselves. Don't take it personally."

"No, take it personally," Sammi snarled. "That's how I meant it."

Ethan's temper flared. "I haven't done anything to you or your team! You can believe that or stuff it — I don't really care! I didn't tip off the Nepalese, but I'll tell you this, though: They're right. This mountain is mean, and it's no place for a little kid. It's not right for Dominic, who could be in danger, and it's not right for the climbers who might have to put *themselves* in danger to rescue him." The well-known smiling face that adorned so many ads for climbing equipment was bright red with anger. "I didn't come into my own mess tent to take this kind of heat! *All I wanted was a lousy cookie!*"

He flung open the pantry chest and yanked out a bag of Oreos to find Dominic's distorted face peering up at him through the clear plastic of a bottle of vinegar.

"Whoa!!"

# CHAPTER SIXTEEN

The weather report sent Base Camp into a frenzy of activity. The forecasting services all seemed to agree. There were clear days ahead, and several of them. The moment for a summit bid was now.

Sneezy filmed Cicero's pep talk, which turned out to be short.

"No panic. Same climb. We're just going to the end this time, that's all."

They dug their crampons into the crisp blue ice of the Khumbu Icefall.

That night they slept at ABC and spent the following day resting on the Cwm.

Cicero had little sympathy for their impatience. "Think of it as a trip to Miami Beach. It's the last heat any of us will feel for a good long time."

The next morning they were up well before the sun in an attempt to be free of the Cwm before the day's eighty-degree temperature swing. Miami Beach was fine for shorts and T-shirts, but not wind suits and heavy gear. Soon they were

EVEREST

back on the Lhotse Face for another torturous slog up steep sheer ice.

It took every ounce of will for Perry to put himself back up there again. Surprisingly, it wasn't quite as terrible as he remembered. How could it be? The acclimatization actually seemed to be working. He could almost breathe, and the effects of altitude felt more like a bad flu than a pile driver to the head. He had promised himself, though, that he was not unhooking his jumar from a fixed line if the entire British royal family wanted to get around him.

In fact, he did get passed, not by royalty, but by the first of several This Way Up summit teams. Ethan, Nestor, and Pasang climbed by on their way to the peak of Lhotse, dead ahead, yet impossibly far away.

Noticing the pure misery on Perry's face, Nestor hefted his ice ax like a microphone and boomed, " 'We have nothing to fear but fear itself!' "

"In that case," Perry panted back. "I should be pretty darn scared."

The other SummitQuest climbers offered their encouragement to Nestor and Pasang as they labored past. No one said a word to Ethan Zaph.

That night at Camp Three, Cicero held classes

THE CLIMB

in Oxygen 101. For the rest of the climb, each SummitQuest team member would wear portable breathing equipment — an oxygen mask and regulator hooked up to a sleek, ultralight cylinder of compressed gas. Tomorrow they would be crossing the important threshold of twenty-five thousand feet. There was no camp there, or even any milestone. But twenty-five thousand feet marked the beginning of Everest's infamous Death Zone.

"Supplemental oxygen *helps* you survive in the Death Zone. Remember I said *helps*. Because nobody, on *any* amount of O's, can last up there for long. Make no mistake — when you go that high, you're dying. Brain cells are disappearing, your heart beats at triple speed, and your blood gets thick like molasses. We're all on borrowed time above twenty-five K. The O's just let you borrow a little more of it, that's all."

Sammi, who included deep-sea diving on her list of extreme hobbies, had no trouble getting used to her oxygen mask. But the boys found them vastly uncomfortable, and even scary. Perry could not get over the feeling that he was suffocating, even though he was getting more oxygen, not less. Dominic found it spooky to hear the sound of his own breathing reverberating in his ears.

Tilt felt the same way. "It's like Darth Vader breath," he complained, tossing his mask aside. "I'll get the hang of it tomorrow."

"You'll get the hang of it *now*," Cicero insisted. "Nobody sleeps till you're totally comfortable in that rig."

Nobody slept anyway. The stakes were getting too high.

www.summathletic.com/everest/southcol

No, they're not astronauts; they're the youngest expedition in the history of Mount Everest in full high-altitude gear, including oxygen. At this point in the climb our heroes might as well be walking on the moon. The atmosphere is virtually unbreathable, and they are far beyond the rescue range of modern technology.

The route to Camp Four is the highest left turn on the planet, an ascending traverse across the Yellow Band — five hundred feet of steep, crumbling limestone. Next comes a rock climb in the sky over the Geneva Spur, a decaying black club overlooking the Cwm by nearly a vertical mile.

THE CLIMB

It is not far now — the South Col, at the edge of Earth's atmosphere at twenty-six thousand feet. This barren wasteland of ice and stone is the site of Camp Four, the last stop before the summit. With nighttime temperatures of eighty below zero in lethal alliance with wind gusts more than one hundred miles per hour, this is not a relaxing place. Yet relax they must. For at midnight, they will walk right into the teeth of the worst conditions the mountain has to offer. **CLICK HERE** to see the SummitQuest climbers at Camp Four trying to grab a scant few hours of sleep before their final test on top of the world.

"I can't sleep," Dominic mumbled into his oxygen mask.

"Who asked you to?" roared Tilt. "I just need you to shut up long enough for *me* to get some rest!"

Perry tried to keep the peace in the close quarters. Due to the difficulty of ferrying equipment this high, the eight SummitQuest climbers were crammed into two three-person tents. "Come on, Tilt. We're all nervous."

This was not strictly true. The others were nervous. Perry Noonan was scared out of his wits.

He was playing a chess game in his head in a vain attempt to divert his mind. But he could get no further than three or four moves before his discomfort and fear brought him back to the Death Zone.

"I'm so pumped," said Sammi, pulling the mask from her face so she could be heard. "I mean, think about it. There's nothing about this moment that isn't extreme. Breathing extreme air in extreme cold and extreme wind, getting ready to take on the ultimate extreme mountain!"

Perry fiddled with his mask. "Who can sleep in this getup?"

Tilt pushed him back down on his sleeping bag. "That's easy for you to say. You don't need rest. You're going to quit before we hit the ridge. *I'm* going the distance tonight so — everybody — shut up!"

Dominic crawled to the entrance. "I'm going to check the radio. See if any of the other teams made the summit today."

Outside, the arctic blast of wind nearly bent him double. Nylon flapped against aluminum poles at such high frequency that Camp Four gave off an electric buzz. The seven-foot walk to the guides' tent seemed like a struggle. He poked his head inside. Dr. Oberman and Sneezy were trying to get some sleep. Cicero and Babu were

at the radio. Babu was the only one not breathing bottled gas. He never climbed with it — not even at the summit.

The stout Sherpa was the first to notice him. "Who's there?"

*I must look like a storm trooper from Star Wars in this oxygen rig,* Dominic reminded himself, pulling the mask aside.

Cicero yanked him in and zipped the flap shut. "You should be sleeping, kid."

Dominic shrugged. Few ever slept on the Col prior to a midnight climb. The conditions, the altitude, and the nervousness seldom allowed it. After a summit push, when the body has had every molecule of strength, will, and, at last, awareness wrung from it — that was the time for sleep. "Did anybody get to the top today?"

Babu shook his head. "The Guamanians are back. They didn't get very far. Some of the Japanese are still out there. They made it to the South Summit before turning around." He added, "But they're doing fine."

No sooner had the words crossed his lips than a barrage of angry words exploded from the radio. It was a full-fledged screaming argument — and definitely not in Japanese.

Cicero ripped off his mask, grabbed the microphone, and boomed, "This is Cap Cicero! Identify yourselves!"

"Cap, it's me — Nestor!" The voice sounded as exhausted as it was enraged. "I'm with Ethan and Pasang! We're above twenty-seven on Lhotse and — somebody messed up! I don't know who — maybe the staff at Base Camp — "

"What's going on out there?" Cicero roared.

"We're out of rope!"

Out of rope! Dominic could hardly believe his ears. There were many reasons for an ascent to fail — a storm, an accident, or the human body just reaching its limit. But to have to turn back because there wasn't enough rope to stretch all the way to the top — that was agony. They were only a few hundred feet below the Lhotse summit!

"Don't do anything stupid!" Cicero ordered in a commanding tone. "You climb without ropes, and somebody's going to slip!"

"But we're *there*, man!" Nestor was moaning. "We're off the ice! No more crampons even! Just a rock gully all the way to the peak!"

"Is Zaph there! Let me talk to Zaph — "

Suddenly, a Sherpa voice — Pasang's — cried, *"Rockfall!"*

There was an audible thud, then Ethan yelled, "Nestor's hit! Grab him!"

"What's going on?" Cicero bellowed into the radio.

His only response was violent rustling and static.

"What's happening? Who's out there?"

Ethan's voice, now distant, screamed, "Nestor! Wake up! *Wake up!*" and then the signal went dead.

# CHAPTER SEVENTEEN

Sneezy and Dr. Oberman weren't sleeping anymore. By this time, the four guides and Dominic were crowded around the small radio. Cicero called all the other expeditions. No one was anywhere near the climbers in trouble. The closest teams were at Camp Four. The Guamanians were exhausted from their failed summit bid, and the Japanese were still on the mountain. SummitQuest alone was in any shape to offer assistance.

"If Nestor's really unconscious," the doctor said grimly, "there's no way two men can get him down the face from that altitude."

"We've got to help him!" exclaimed Dominic.

Cicero glared at him. "You're going to stay here and sit tight with the others. We'll look for them."

Sneezy was surprised. "All of us? Shouldn't somebody stick with the kids?"

Cicero shook his head. "Zaph's climbing without O's. Maybe he can handle himself, but I doubt he's got the strength for a rescue. We don't want to drag ourselves all the way out there just to be caught short."

Babu nodded. "We'll have to traverse to the face until we hit their fixed line. Then we can head up the ropes and catch them descending."

"If they're not doing it headfirst at sixty miles an hour," Sneezy said pointedly.

Dominic nodded. "I'll tell the others."

The team leader grabbed his arm. "You know what this means, right?"

And Dominic did. There would be no summit bid tonight. Even if Cicero and the guides could effect a quick rescue and be back at Camp Four by midnight, they would be far too fatigued to set out for the top of Everest. In all likelihood, the team would have to retreat to ABC, or even Base Camp, to wait for another weather window.

He swallowed hard. Everest was fickle. They might not get another chance.

Dominic didn't hesitate. It was the unwritten rule of mountaineering: A rescue takes precedence over everything. Even a shot at the pinnacle of the world.

"Go!"

"The radio!"

Pasang watched as Nestor's walkie-talkie skittered down the Lhotse Face and disappeared from view. By the time it reached the Western Cwm more than a mile below, it would be traveling at unimaginable speed.

He helped Ethan turn Nestor over on his back — not an easy task at over twenty-seven thousand feet. Ethan flipped up the journalist's oxygen mask and listened tensely.

"He's still breathing. Thank God."

The boulder that hit Nestor had come out of nowhere, a flying projectile the size of a microwave oven. It had struck him squarely in the backpack, momentarily dislodging him from the mountain and leaving him hanging from the fixed ropes.

"Breathing now," Pasang agreed. "But what next?"

It was a good question. Near the summit, the western ramparts of Lhotse straightened to near vertical, and the treacherous face sloped upward at eighty degrees in places. For two climbers to get an unconscious companion down even as far as Camp Three would be impossible.

Ethan thought it over. The walkie-talkie was gone. Nobody knew they were in trouble. Descent wasn't an option, so . . .

"We'll go up," he decided.

"Without rope?" the Sherpa exclaimed. "One slip and — "

"Down is *ice*," Ethan argued. "Up is rock.

Down is far; up is close. We can practically crawl to the summit from here, dragging Nestor behind us. From there, we can take the ridge down to the South Col. One of the teams is bound to have a doctor at Camp Four."

"No fixed ropes on ridge, either," Pasang pointed out. "Cornices. Very dangerous."

"But possible. It's Nestor's only chance." He slapped the unconscious journalist's cheeks. "Come on, buddy, wake up!"

Nestor did not stir.

"All right," Pasang assented finally. "We go to summit."

Tilt stood on the black rocks of the South Col and gazed bleakly at the sun going down on the Western Cwm. It was one of the truly spectacular sights on Planet Earth, but he saw none of it.

*Stinkin' Nestor!*

Every time he thought about it, white-hot rage boiled through his brain.

*Why this? Why now?*

When Tilt thought ahead to the future, *every single thing in it* depended on this summit bid! The summit *was* his future. And it was *happening!* From here at twenty-six thousand feet, the top seemed so close he could practically hit it with a spitball. . . .

*And then that clown has to go and get himself nailed by a rock!*

He had always known Cicero was a jerk, but he never would have believed the mountaineering legend could be such a sucker. Why would he jeopardize the whole expedition just to rescue Nestor?

*Nothing against Nestor, but why can't somebody else save him? His own expedition — they should be doing this! Not Cap! Not SummitQuest!*

But Nestor's This Way Up teammates were all at Camp Two or lower. A group had started up the Cwm to help him on the way down. But by then this weather window would be history. There might be another; there might not. It would be decided by pure luck.

*Not something you want to stake your whole future on.*

The attack came from behind. Arms reached around his sides, and someone wrestled him down. Shocked and afraid, Tilt hit the rocky ground and rolled free. His assailant was a Sherpa in full climbing gear, including oxygen mask and goggles. The man scrambled up and made another run at Tilt.

"What do you want?" bawled Tilt.

But the Sherpa kept coming, stumbling like a

punch-drunk boxer. Terrified, Tilt backed away, casting a nervous eye over his shoulder. He was very near the point where the flat South Col rounded into the steep Lhotse Face — a deadly fall.

"Get away from me!"

The Sherpa reached for him. Then, as if the effort of lifting his arms had sapped all his remaining strength, he collapsed to his knees. A moment later, he was on all fours, gasping into his mask.

Light dawned on Tilt. *This guy isn't fighting me! He's so exhausted he can't even stand!*

On Cicero's orders, the teen climbers had moved to the guides' tent in order to keep an eye on the radio. Tilt hustled the Sherpa inside and pulled off the mask and goggles.

"Pasang!" cried Dominic in dismay. The normally confident climber was shivering uncontrollably.

They wrapped Pasang in blankets. Perry made him a cup of hot chocolate to warm him up.

"How's Nestor?" probed Dominic.

"Nestor very bad," the Sherpa reported gravely. "I think maybe will die on mountain."

"What are you talking about?" cried Sammi. "Aren't they bringing him down?"

Pasang looked blank.

Dominic grabbed his arm. "Cap, Babu, Sneezy, and Andrea left a few hours ago to help you guys up on the face."

The Sherpa put his head in his hands and moaned aloud. "Very big mistake! Very bad!" His eyes were filled with horror. "Ethan say, 'No safe climb down face. Climb summit and down ridge.' "

There was a breathless pause as the terrible truth sank in. Cicero and the guides were searching for Ethan and Nestor on the Lhotse Face. And all this time, the two had summited and were somewhere along the northeast ridge. It was a colossal mixup — one with consequences that could prove to be deadly.

A roar of laughter broke the stunned silence. "This is just fantastic!" Tilt exploded. "We throw away our summit chance so Cap can stage a rescue, but there's no one there to rescue anymore! Tell you what — when we get back to the States, we can go to Hollywood and sell the movie rights to *Climbing with Morons!*"

"Come on, Tilt," Perry said feelingly. "Nestor could die up there."

"No just Nestor!" Pasang's horror story had one final wrinkle. After hauling Nestor's unconscious body to the summit, they had started down Lhotse's northeast ridge. Pasang took Ethan's pack, and Ethan carried Nestor piggyback style. It was an unbelievable feat of strength — especially for someone climbing without oxygen. But after an hour of descent, Ethan had collapsed. It was not a misstep or a fall. The famous young alpinist had just run completely out of steam.

"I try give Ethan my O's," Pasang went on, tears trickling down his frost-nipped cheeks. "But he say no — go Camp Four. Find Cap Cicero."

"If he wanted to climb with Cap, he shouldn't have quit SummitQuest!" Tilt snapped irritably.

"Cap has no hard feelings about that," Sammi countered. "He was ready to go after Nestor and Ethan. He thinks he's doing it right now, but he's in the wrong place!"

And then Dominic said, quietly but firmly, "We'll do it."

# CHAPTER EIGHTEEN

"Do what?" Perry looked at him in alarm. "You don't mean — "

"We'll climb up the ridge and get Nestor and Ethan."

"Oh, no, you don't," warned Tilt. "I signed on to climb one mountain — Everest. Nobody said anything about Lhotse!"

Sammi got in his face, pressing her oxygen mask right up against his. "I'm on to you, Crowley. You're a jerk — but not a big enough jerk to let people die."

Dominic hunched over the radio. "Cap. Cap, come in please."

Cicero's voice came out of the tinny speaker. The team leader sounded totally spent. "Doesn't look good, kid. We've been on the face for three hours, and there's no sign of them. I think maybe they fell."

Dominic took a deep breath. "Brace yourself, Cap — they're on the northeast ridge." He explained the latest developments from Pasang. "Nestor's out cold, and Ethan — I guess he just

THE CLIMB

kind of hit the wall. We're going to climb up and see if we can bring them down."

"No!!" barked Cicero. "Stay put! We'll come after them!"

Dominic looked pointedly at Pasang. The Sherpa shook his head. Two hours minimum for the guides to return; perhaps another hour to recuperate before starting up the ridge. Nestor and Ethan didn't have that much time.

"We think that might take too long," Dominic said carefully. "Nestor's hurt bad, and Ethan's got no oxygen high in the Death Zone."

"That's an unknown ridge, and there's maybe half an hour of daylight left! I absolutely forbid — "

Sammi reached around the radio and pulled out the battery pack. The set went dead. "These things are so unreliable at altitude," she said calmly.

Their first stop was the equipment dump between the two tents. There, they loaded up — oxygen bottles, a spare breathing rig for Ethan, and helmet lamps. Perry was throwing heavy coils of rope over his shoulders and around his neck.

"Whoa, Perry," called Sammi. "We're not climbing to Tibet, you know."

"There's not a single fixed line on that ridge!" Perry shot back, stuffing his knapsack with ice screws. "If we don't do this right, somebody is going to end up dead!"

She squinted at his face, barely visible behind goggles and mask. *He's petrified,* she thought, *but maybe that's a good thing.* Perry's fear made him a mediocre mountaineer, but it had also turned him into a master of ropes, pegs, screws, and pitons. He had trained himself to belay an elephant — not a bad guy to have around when the chips were down.

Pasang had to be physically restrained from coming with them. "You won't make it. You're too tired," Dominic told him kindly but firmly. "We can rescue two, but not three." At last, the exhausted Sherpa agreed to wait for them in the tent.

For safety, they roped themselves together in pairs — Sammi and Perry, Tilt and Dominic. It was not yet dark, but the temperature gauge on Dominic's watch read forty-nine degrees below zero. They could only guess at the windchill.

The first obstacle of their ascent was a towering triangular wall of wind-scoured ice. It stretched from the Col fifty stories up to the northeast ridge, which began at its tip.

THE CLIMB

Perry tried without success to place a screw near its base. "The ice is barely an inch thick. I don't think it's safe."

Sammi front-pointed past him. "You know how to make it safe?" she called. "Don't fall!"

They were twenty feet up when Tilt's crampons lost their hold of the thin rime. He slid down the wall, and as he did, Perry's screws popped out of the ice one by one. Tilt was unhurt as he tumbled to the Col — but only because the accident hadn't taken place four hundred feet higher.

*"You stupid idiot!!"* he roared, not at his companions, but at Lhotse itself. "I wouldn't even be climbing here if it wasn't for lousy Ethan Zaph, whose record is going to stand forever! I can't break it because I'm too busy rescuing *him!*"

They climbed on, determined to reach the ridge before darkness fell. Perry inched along, stubbornly laying down a line. The others said nothing. They knew that the rope was practically useless. Anything heavier than a dictionary would rip the screws clear out of the mountain.

*But it's a fixed route,* he reassured himself. It took his mind off the truth — that he was hanging off the fourth highest mountain on the planet, supported by nothing more than the half-inch of front points he could plant in the wall. Somewhere much deeper inside him, he was repeating Sammi's words: *Don't fall . . . don't fall . . .*

A crampon shattered the thin layer of verglas, leaving him hanging on to his ax for dear life. Frantically, he kicked at the face searching for a purchase. But every stab of his foot broke the ice up even more, leaving nothing but inhospitable naked rock.

"You okay, Perry?" Sammi called down at him.

*No, I'm not okay!* he wanted to shriek back. *Three hundred feet off the Col, and I've got nowhere to stick a crampon! It's like trying to climb a moonbeam!*

But he knew that was the Death Zone talking. At extreme altitude, the brain wasn't receiving enough oxygen to work properly. That was why so many smart mountaineers made bad decisions in the Himalayas.

*Come on, Perry,* he exhorted himself. *Think!*

Carefully, he scraped his crampons along the exposed stone until he found a tiny ledge about the thickness of a pea. Pressing his side-points down on it, he heaved himself up to more stable ice. *Kick, kick, thunk,* and he was on the way up again.

Night fell, forcing them to ascend to the apex

of the triangle by the eerie glow of their helmet lamps. Once on the ridge, the going was easier, but no less hazardous. The feel of their crampons crunching into hard-packed snow filled them with confidence. But that same snow had been wind-blown to form massive cornices. It was impossible to tell where solid rock ended and unsupported cornice began. Break through, and your fate would be a mile-and-a-half plunge to the Kang-shung glacier far below.

Every step drew them farther into the Death Zone. The effort of putting one foot in front of the other became less an act of mountaineering and more an exercise in suffering. Even with bottled oxygen, breathing became gasping.

*Ten steps, then a break,* Sammi ordered herself. Soon she was resting every seven. Then every five.

For nearly a thousand vertical feet, they slogged over rock and corniced snow. Notches in the ridge created small cliffs, ranging in height from ten to fifteen feet. At home, they would have been routine scrambles. Here, more than five miles above sea level, they presented punishing obstacles that left the four sobbing with sheer fatigue.

Agonizingly slowly, Perry twisted screws into the bulletproof ice and roped the jagged steps.

"Hurry up, Noonan!" shouted Tilt from below. "We're freezing to death down here!"

Anywhere else, his words would be an exaggeration. But the altimeter on Dominic's watch read 27,479 feet, and the air temperature had dropped to −66°F. Despite their exhaustion, Tilt, Sammi, and Dominic danced on the spot as they waited for Perry. Frostbite rarely struck a mountaineer in motion; it was the standing around that caused the extremities to freeze.

"Where are Ethan and Nestor?" shivered Sammi, pounding her mitts together to maintain circulation. "We're only a few hundred feet below the summit."

"The famous Ethan Zaph," growled Tilt. "When we're finished rescuing him, I'm going to throw him off the mountain!"

Perry was near the top of the notch, looking to place one final screw. "I can't find any ice!" he called down to the others. Here the wind had blasted the ridge down to bare shale. He looked around for another route up. The gash in the mountain continued on both sides as far as the glow of his helmet lamp would allow him to see.

The frustration grew inside him, overshadowing even his fear. A human life depended on their success — two lives, probably. How could they turn back now?

THE CLIMB

"Use the piton!" Dominic called from below.

"I didn't bring any!" Perry cried, beginning to lose control. He'd assumed the entire route would be covered with ice. It was a mistake — *his* mistake. And because of it, two people were going to die. . . .

"Your *uncle's* piton!" Dominic insisted.

*Oh.* Perry hesitated. *That piton.* Uncle Joe had sent five guys to the wilds of Alberta to recover that dumb peg. It was meant for the summit of Everest, not some no-name notch on Lhotse!

*He'll be furious if I waste it.*

At that moment, it occurred to him how crazy that was. He was hanging off a rock a zillion feet up in a windchill of minus infinity — and he was worried about what Uncle Joe might say?

"No," he said aloud into the punishing wind. Then, louder: "No!" The thoughts came in an emotional flood, washing away the tension of the climb. *I love you, Uncle Joe, but if I'm so spooked by you that I'd let two people die — that's just plain wrong!*

He pulled off his small knapsack and reached inside, coming up with the twenty-five-year-old peg. Fifteen thousand dollars — more than its weight in gold, probably. That's what Uncle Joe said it had cost to get it back — a weathered, rusty piece of iron.

*Well, easy come, easy go!* Perry found a good crack and hammered the piton in with the flat end of his ice ax. Then he strung the rope through its ring and heaved himself up to the top of the step.

And screamed.

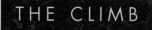

# CHAPTER NINETEEN

Sammi, Dominic, and Tilt jumared up the rope as fast as the altitude would allow their weary arms to move. One by one, they scrambled over the prow of shale. There they found Perry, on his hands and knees, dry-heaving into his respirator. A few feet in front of him, sprawled on the rocks, lay the dead body of a climber.

Dominic felt his legs begin to wobble. The victim seemed to be male, although it was impossible to tell. The face was partially mummified by the blistering cold, flesh receding to reveal the contours of a human skull. A death mask in the sky.

For the SummitQuest climbers, already at the outer limit of their endurance, the shock of it stopped them in their tracks. They knew that there were many such grisly sights in the Himalayas — alpinists who lost their lives so high up that their bodies could never be safely recovered. But to crest a rise and find yourself staring directly into the face of death was something no mountaineer could ever be prepared for. Even Tilt was visibly

EVEREST

shaken, his eyes wide with horror, wheezing into his oxygen system.

"It's Nestor!" Perry was blubbering. "We're too late! He's dead!"

Sammi grabbed him by his shoulders. "It can't be! This guy's been here for years! Look at him!"

"No!" He shook her off angrily, but he knew she was right. So much deformity could not possibly have happened so quickly. Yet this news, which should have heartened him, only wrenched even more sobs from him.

"Shut up! Shut up!" Tilt was yelling more from fear than anger. *If this wimp doesn't stop crying, I'm going to lose it!* "It's just a dead guy with freezer burn!"

"There was a team up here in the mid-nineties," Dominic babbled, none too steady himself. "Italians, I think. This could be one of — "

"You shut up, too!" Tilt roared. "If you all don't shut up, I swear I'll — "

And then they heard it, faint but crystal clear — a distant voice calling, "Hey!"

Sammi's keen eyes spotted the dim amber ghost of a fading helmet lamp, a half-mile farther up the ridge. "Ethan," she breathed.

The body forgotten, they rushed along the jagged slope with the renewed vigor of climbers on a mission. They stopped only to remove their crampons for better progress on the bare rock. Here, any snow that touched Lhotse was immediately flung out over the Kangshung glacier by wrenching wind gusts that threatened to dislodge the rescuers from the mountain.

The four bent into the gale and sped up. They had seen death; it had almost overwhelmed them. But now they reached down deep and found hidden reserves of strength because they didn't want that fate for their fellow climbers.

"Ethan!" shouted Sammi.

"Over here." Now the response was close. It was a sound they had not heard before — that famous voice, hollow with exhaustion and defeat.

And suddenly, the two lost climbers were right in front of them. Dominic hardly recognized the top young mountaineer in the world. Ethan sat cross-legged, meek and trembling over Nestor's unmoving form. The journalist's face was white as chalk under his oxygen mask.

Ethan regarded Dominic without recognition at first. Then, "You! Are you everywhere or something? How could you be — ?" He seemed to lose his train of thought partway through the question. He had been in the Death Zone without oxygen for more than eleven hours.

Sammi and Perry hooked up the spare breathing rig and placed the mask over Ethan's mouth and nose. He perked up immediately. "We couldn't wake him up," he said, pointing at Nestor. "We were at the summit — wait, no. On the face — no — " His oxygen-starved brain could not seem to organize his thoughts.

"I'd be getting ready for a summit bid if it wasn't for you," Tilt accused, which only confused Ethan further.

Sammi and Perry rolled Nestor onto his side, allowing Dominic to turn the flow on his gas regulator up to four liters per minute — the maximum.

The back of Nestor's wind suit and his knapsack were crusted with tiny red crystals. "What's that?" asked Perry.

"Blood," replied Sammi. "Frozen blood." She turned to Dominic, perplexed. "He was hit by rockfall. The injuries should be mostly internal, right?"

Dominic tried to remove the knapsack. It wouldn't budge. Frowning, Dominic zipped it open and fumbled around inside. His mitts fell on a coil of some kind of wire. He pulled it out to realize he was holding Nestor's summit Slinky. The unimaginable cold of the Death Zone had made the thin metal so brittle that it shattered in Dominic's hands.

There was something else in there. He adjusted his helmet lamp and shone it inside the small pack. The others gathered around. In an instant, the nature of Nestor's injury became completely clear.

"Oh, my God," gasped Perry.

The journalist had been climbing with his crampons in his knapsack in the rock gully near the top of Lhotse. The falling stone had struck the pack, driving the razor-sharp crampon points through the fabric of his wind suit, into his back.

"Ouch," commented Tilt.

"It's like being stabbed by ten knives," added Sammi with a wince.

Dominic tried again to yank the knapsack free. But the crampon points were in so deep that Nestor's entire body was stuck to the pack and would not separate from it. Finally, Sammi, Perry, and Dominic held on to him, while Tilt, the strongest, heaved with all his might.

"Aaaaaaaah!!" Nestor howled in pain as the crampons were torn from his flesh.

Tilt staggered in reverse and went down, the knapsack clutched in his arms. Nestor got up on all fours. "My back! My back!"

"Nestor, it's Dominic! Dominic Alexis!" Breathlessly, he tried to explain what had happened during the time the journalist had been unconscious. "You're two hundred feet below the summit of Lhotse and you've got ten stab wounds in your back. We've got to get you down to Dr. Oberman."

"Can you walk?" asked Sammi.

With great effort and much assistance, Nestor struggled to his feet. "I'll never make it," he moaned, panting from the effort. "It hurts so much!"

"He's lucky he's at this altitude," Sammi whispered to Perry. "Blood's thicker than mud up here. At sea level, he would have bled to death by now."

"At sea level, they would have sent an ambulance," Perry retorted.

The good news was that Ethan could now walk on his own. Nestor was another story. With Sammi supporting the right arm and Dominic under the left, he could barely put one foot in front of the other. They were facing a third of a mile of vertical descent down to Camp Four. On the tricky and perilous ridge, it might as well have been a light-year.

They checked their oxygen equipment, replacing empty bottles and clearing ice from masks and regulator tubes. It was decided that Sammi, Perry, and Dominic would all rope themselves to Nestor. With luck, the three of them might be able to guide the injured journalist through the tough journey ahead. Tilt alone would handle Ethan.

"You're lucky I don't handle you right off a cliff, superstar," Tilt grumbled, tethering himself to Ethan's harness.

Progress was slow, and maneuvering Nestor down the many drop-offs proved to be time-consuming and difficult. Soon the ridge was snow-covered again, and they had to stop to reaffix their crampons. The menacing cornices called for extra-special care, which delayed them even more.

Tilt spent the entire descent griping at Ethan. "The great Ethan Zaph. Don't make me laugh. If you're so great, how come we had to rescue your sorry butt?"

Poor Ethan had no strength to defend himself. Baby steps down the ridge were all he could manage.

*Me!* he lamented. *The strongest young climber ever!*

He was depressed, but grateful. He knew that these kids had just saved his life. The little guy especially — *I was wrong about him.* Few could function at this altitude, let alone take charge. For a thirteen-year-old to show this kind of poise and ability in the Death Zone was flat-out unbelievable.

Suddenly, the snow beneath his feet disintegrated. In an instant of exquisite terror, he realized that he was not on the ridge at all, but on a cornice curling improbably far out over the Kangshung Face. And then gravity took him and flung him downward.

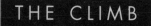

THE CLIMB

# CHAPTER TWENTY

"Your ax!" bellowed Tilt, frozen with fear. In a few seconds, the rope would play out, and more than two hundred pounds of plummeting climber would pull him off the mountain.

Ethan reached for his ice tool — one *last chance!* But as he fumbled for the handle, it was already too late. He was sliding down the rock, picking up speed, his mind empty of all thoughts but one: *When you fall a mile and a half, are you still alive when you hit the bottom?*

Tilt Crowley threw himself to the snow, locked his arms around the biggest boulder he could find, and hung on for dear life.

"Oof!!"

The jolt slammed his face against hard granite. The force on his harness was so great that his entire body was lifted up in the air. Everything went momentarily black. But he held on to the rock, to the ridge, to Lhotse, to life.

His eyes fluttered open. He had done it! He could feel Ethan's weight dangling at the other end of the rope. The question remained: Was it *dead* weight? Had the boy survived the fall?

EVEREST

A faint cry from below. "Help!"

Sammi and Dominic grabbed for the rope, but Tilt pushed them aside. "I don't need *you!*" He planted his crampons and got to his feet, leaning away from the precipice, two hands on the taut line. "Hey, Zaph!" he roared triumphantly out over the abyss. "You call yourself strong? You don't know the meaning of the word! *This* is strong!" Single-handedly, he began hauling in the line. Sammi and Dominic joined in.

Minutes later, a trembling Ethan, pop-eyed and ashen-faced, crested the ridge. He collapsed into Tilt's arms, gasping and wheezing.

"Settle down," Tilt ordered in an irritated tone. "I don't even like you."

"You don't like anybody," grinned Sammi. She put an arm around Tilt's shoulders. "That was amazing — and I don't amaze easily."

"The greatest belay I've ever seen," added Perry.

"Big deal," snorted Tilt. "By the time the press gets through with it, it'll be Zaph the hero belaying the rest of us by his nose hairs."

It would be a solid hour before Ethan would release his death grip on Tilt's arm.

At exactly 10:30 P.M., the alarm on Dominic's watch began beeping. A rueful laugh escaped

THE CLIMB

him. In another life, on another mountain, that was the signal to wake up and get ready for their assault on the peak of Everest. It was time to melt ice to make tea and hot chocolate. Time to force down oatmeal and Summit bars, energy for the climb ahead.

Everest. It seemed distant somehow. As if it had never been their original goal, and the plan had always been a perilous rescue on the upper reaches of Lhotse.

*Attempted* rescue, he corrected himself. By no means was this a done deal. They were well below twenty-seven thousand feet now, but Ethan was flagging and Nestor was deteriorating badly. Dominic was pretty sure that if it weren't for the physical support of his fellow climbers, the journalist would have lacked even the strength to stand up.

No one noticed when Nestor began to gasp, sucking hungrily for oxygen that was no longer there. He tried to sound the alert, but he didn't have the air. All that came out were two croaking syllables: "Help me." He collapsed to the snow.

Sammi checked for a blockage in his breathing tube, but it was clear. Perry checked the gauge on Nestor's oxygen bottle. "Empty!"

"We're such idiots!" Sammi exclaimed. "He's

drawing O's twice as fast as the rest of us! Of course he's going to run out first!"

Dominic fumbled desperately inside his pack, looking for a spare cylinder. *This is my fault!* he thought frantically, *I should have known better! I should have seen it coming.*

He slapped the new bottle into place, and Sammi hooked it into the regulator. They watched expectantly. Nestor's breathing stabilized, but he did not come to.

For twenty precious minutes, they tried to wake him, shaking him, slapping him, screaming in his ears, and even pressing snow against his cheeks. But in a windchill approaching one hundred degrees below zero, twenty minutes of inactivity was more than a delay; it was a foolhardy risk to life and limb. In the Death Zone, climbing was the body's natural heater, its last line of defense against frostbite and hypothermia. They had to keep going.

Tilt grabbed Nestor under the arms; Sammi took his legs. For a while, the ridge unfolded gently before them, and they made good time. Nestor's labored footsteps had been so slow that they were actually moving faster this way. Then they rounded a bend, and the lights of their helmet lamps seemed to disappear into blackness.

Dominic looked down. They were five hundred feet above the South Col, at the apex of the triangular ice wall.

Sammi shone her lamp over the steep slope. "Oh, boy."

Perry was the first to panic. "We'll never get him down this!"

"Wait!" Ethan pointed. "Fixed line!"

Tilt shook his head. "Worthless." He yanked the top screw out of the ice. The entire rope dislodged from the mountain, anchors popping down its full length.

The conference was short.

"We'll have to leave him," Sammi decided. "The guides must be back at Camp Four by now. Maybe Andrea can climb up here and give him a shot or something."

"Nestor doesn't have that kind of time," Dominic argued. "We've got to get him down *now*."

Tilt turned on him angrily. "How, shrimp? You know why they don't bring dead bodies back from the upper mountain? Because it's impossible! And unconscious guys are dead guys in training!"

"He's right," said Perry sadly. "To get off this rock, you've got to *walk* off."

Even Ethan agreed there was nothing they

could do for his teammate anymore. "We'll leave him and go for help."

Dominic was not swayed. Who knew for sure if Dr. Oberman was on the Col? And even if she was, it would still mean a long climb down, a longer one back up again, and then a difficult descent with Nestor.

His eyes fell on the dislodged rope, which lay before Tilt, a loose ice screw flopped on its side. "We'll lower him down."

"We don't have enough rope," Perry protested.

Dominic pulled the tether cord out of his harness. "Tie them all together. We can make it."

"We can't," Tilt insisted. "We're not even close. That's got to be five hundred feet!"

But Dominic was adamant. "We'll get him down. I swear."

# CHAPTER TWENTY-ONE

They knotted the nylon lines together and tied one end to Nestor's harness. Then they eased the journalist over the top. Dominic followed on his front points and ice ax.

Sammi looked at him dubiously. "I hope you know what you're doing. You're still way short."

"Trust me," Dominic promised, and was gone.

Tilt and Perry let out the rope, and Nestor slid slowly down the wall of ice. Dominic kept pace. *Kick, Kick, thunk. Kick, kick, thunk . . .*

They had been descending for only about twenty minutes when Nestor's progress abruptly halted.

"That's the end!" Sammi shouted down from the ridge.

Dominic pushed his mask aside and bellowed, "Give me a minute!" He looked around and found his helmet lamp shining right at it, exactly where he'd expected it to be. There, maybe ten feet to his left, was another fixed line. It had taken Perry three pitches to reach the top of the triangular wall. This was the second length. Still another waited below.

EVEREST

Front-pointing efficiently, Dominic traversed to the rope and yanked it free of the mountain's thin rind, sending ice screws tumbling down to the Col. Now came the hard part — keeping Nestor secure while adding on the new length. He plastered his shoulder to the slope, wedging the journalist in place as he worked. .

"What's going on?" came Sammi's call.

Dominic fastened the knot. "Reel it in!" he ordered.

High above, confusion turned to dismay as Tilt and Perry hauled the slackened rope effortlessly upward.

"What did he do with Nestor?" Tilt muttered in consternation. "What's going on?"

Sammi watched in bewilderment as the double fisherman's knot rose into the glow of her helmet lamp. Her eyes widened in sudden understanding. "He found the second rope!"

"And there's another one after that!" Perry exclaimed excitedly.

"Unbelievable!" breathed Ethan, energized by the genius of the thirteen-year-old's plan. He flipped up his mask. "Go, Dominic! Do it, kid!"

When they felt Nestor's weight on the line, Tilt and Perry resumed lowering the rope. Below, Dominic continued his descent alongside the journalist's inert form. The work was hard — front-

THE CLIMB

pointing with only one ice tool was more difficult than with two. His right arm and shoulder throbbed with pain, but inside he was celebrating. *It's going to work. We're going to get Nestor to the Col.* From there, he wasn't sure of the next step, but he was confident his friend would be in good hands. *If Andrea can revive him, Cap and Babu can get him down. He's got a chance. A helicopter can land as high as twenty-thousand feet. It isn't easy, but it's possible.*

So absorbed was he in figuring the angles of the rescue that he barely heard Sammi yelling. He was too far away to make out her exact words, but he realized that Nestor's descent had been halted once more.

His eyes scanned the ice for the final fixed rope. It wasn't there.

The realization was like a cannon shot to the pit of his stomach. There was no rope. It had fallen, or blown away in the permanent gale of the Death Zone. He checked the altimeter on his watch: 26,148. They were still well over a hundred feet above the Col. And Nestor was stranded, dangling like a yo-yo on a string.

Dominic's head filled with a blizzard of bad ideas. *I'll front-point down and look for help!* But what if there was no help? *I'll climb back up again!* What good would that do?

His eyes filled with tears. Maybe they were right — the people who said he didn't belong here. Oh, sure, he could handle himself physically on the mountain. But what about *mentally*? The pressure to do the right thing when someone's life hung in the balance. Was any thirteen-year-old ever ready for that emotional roller-coaster ride?

The last words hung meaningfully in his thoughts. Roller-coaster ride . . .

*Roller-coaster ride!*

With a deep sense of purpose, he sat Nestor upright on the slope, and maneuvered himself behind, wrapping his arms around the journalist's waist as if the two of them were seated in tandem on a toboggan. In fact, that image was exactly Dominic's plan. It was, in climbing lingo, a glissade — a controlled slide.

*Well, this won't be very controlled, but it's Nestor's only chance.*

Control was a pretty big concern here because the Col was only 150 yards wide. Veering too far to the left would mean a four-thousand-foot drop over the Lhotse Face. A mistake to the right would send them screaming down the Kangshung.

With trembling hands, Dominic drew his brother's vial of Dead Sea sand out of his wind-suit collar. "If you're really magic," he whispered, "now's the time." And with that, he drew back his ax and cut the rope.

He dug the tool into the ice, dragging it behind them in an attempt to control their speed. It worked for the first thirty feet or so, but then gravity took over, and the mountain ripped it violently from his hand. With monstrous acceleration, they rocketed down the steep slope. He felt the wind rip the helmet lamp from his head and toss it contemptuously over the Kangshung Face. Clamping his arms around Nestor, he hung on as the ripples of ice passed beneath them at horrifying velocity.

He fought down an impulse to dig in his crampons to slow the slide. At this pace, the move would only catapult him straight up and send him tumbling to his death. *Hang in there,* he urged himself. He couldn't begin to imagine their speed — eighty miles an hour? Ninety? The altimeter on his watch was flying like the tenths-of-a-second timer on an NBA clock.

The roaring in his ears drowned out the howling of the wind, and his vision began to darken at the corners. "Stay awake!" he screamed at himself, as if the act of yelling might somehow keep him from losing consciousness. But he was fading, his eyes actually closing, when the rocks of the South Col seized his momentum and used it to bounce him around like a Ping-Pong ball.

The instant Sammi saw the two helmet lamps speeding down the wall, she knew.

"Hey!" cried Perry in alarm. "The rope went slack!"

Ethan stared at the ghostly circles of light flying down the mountain. "They fell!"

"That's not it!" exclaimed Sammi as the lamps accelerated in perfect lockstep. "They're *sliding!*"

"That shrimp," said Tilt, shaking his head. "He's crazier than *you* are!"

They watched, transfixed, as one of the lamps suddenly somersaulted away from the other, careening wildly before it disappeared down the Kangshung Face.

"What was — ?" Perry let his voice trail off into the gut-tightening silence. Even the labored sounds of the oxygen gear shut down as the team held its collective breath, paralyzed with dread. At that moment, the answer to Perry's unfinished question seemed pretty clear. They had just seen one of their friends — Nestor or Dominic — plunge to a terrible end.

Tilt heaved himself over the precipice and began front-pointing furiously down the ice. "I'm going down there."

"Me first!" Sammi was hot on his heels.

"What about Ethan?" asked Perry.

But the revitalized Ethan was already on his way down. Perry had no choice but to follow.

# CHAPTER TWENTY-TWO

Pain.

That was Dominic's next reality. His aching body throbbed all over. His mother's words came to mind, repeated often to her climbing men: "You'll break every bone in your body!"

*Well, Mom, you were right. I finally did it.*

No. That wasn't so. While he hurt just about everywhere, he didn't seem to be *badly* hurt anywhere. Just one big bruise from head to toe.

*Nothing broken, everything still attached.* He sprang up.

The powerful beam from a helmet lamp almost knocked him over again. He squinted below the light until he could make out the gawking face of Cap Cicero, plainly amazed to see him alive at all, let alone upright.

In the space of a split second, the team leader's face went from surprise to joy to blind rage. "You little maniac! You know how many climbers would have tried that slide? One! The craziest one! And I'm looking right at him — "

"Where's Nestor?" Dominic interrupted urgently.

"Andrea's got him. This Way Up has a rescue team on its way to the Col."

Dominic watched as the doctor directed Babu and Sneezy to carry the unconscious journalist to the tent.

"He's got ten crampon punctures in his back," he advised her. "He's probably hypoxic, too. And you'd better check for frostbite."

She stared at him and then blinked. "Dominic — the old monk at Thyangboche — the vision — "

"Huh?" he asked. After the night's rescue, their visit to the monastery seemed as if it had happened in another life.

"You've got — " The doctor was practically stammering. "You've got shiny coils all around you!"

Dominic looked down to find the remains of Nestor's Slinky hanging off his wind-suit — silver metal spirals that glistened in the artificial light. The strange lama's prediction — they had called it a hallucination. And yet it had come true.

Cicero had no time for reminiscences. "What about the others?"

Dominic pointed south, where four dim circles of light inched down the invisible wall like night sprites descending from the sky. "Ethan Zaph is the fourth."

The team leader frowned. "How nervous should I be?"

"The ice is too thin, and they've got no ropes, and — " Dominic thought it over. Sure, it was a nasty climb. But compared to all they'd been through that endless night, it was a walk in the park. "They'll make it," he said confidently.

If only he felt the same way about Nestor.

Nestor's ordeal was far from over. At Camp Four, Dr. Oberman stitched up the wounds on his back and gave him a heavy dose of antibiotics to ward off infection. He did not regain consciousness.

The team of This Way Up Sherpas arrived at three A.M. They rested briefly and set out at first light, carrying Nestor in a Gamow bag folded inside a two-person tent. Pasang and Ethan descended with them to assist in the rescue.

Late in the day, the This Way Up climbers arrived at ABC to learn that a rare and risky helicopter evacuation had been set up for the lower Cwm, just beyond Camp One at the top of the Icefall. Cicero and the team were on the Lhotse Face when it happened. They held their breath as they watched, knowing well that the chopper was flying at the very upper edge of its range. At 19,500 feet, the air was too thin to provide the rotor blades with much lift.

The young alpinists watched in agony as the

helicopter had to abort its first two approaches. Then, on the third try, the pilot managed to hover three feet off the glacier — low enough for the injured journalist to be loaded aboard.

Sixty seconds later, the chopper was a tiny dot in the sky. Nestor was on his way to a hospital in Kathmandu.

Only then did SummitQuest start descending — and breathing — again.

The mood at Base Camp was somber for the next two days, and it wasn't just because of the tense vigil by the satellite phone waiting for news of Nestor.

The weather had deteriorated badly. On the summit ridge, a howling blizzard was dumping four feet of snow on already treacherous ground. The weather satellites predicted that it would go on for at least a week.

Babu and some of the other Sherpas thought this might be the onset of the summer monsoon. If they were right, climbing season was over.

"Stick a fork in us," Sammi predicted gloomily. "We're done."

The thought that their summit chances might be finished had sent Tilt's mood into a tailspin. Since returning from the Icefall, he had left his sleeping bag only to eat his meals in stony silence. He had not spoken except to scream at Perry for being "too happy."

"I'm happy I'm not dead!" Perry shot back through the flurries that fell over Base Camp. "And I'm happy I might not get another chance to be dead!"

"You'll be dead if you don't shut up," Tilt promised. "And it won't take any mountain to do it."

Could SummitQuest really be over? Dominic checked with Cicero several times each day.

"Fifty-fifty, kid," was the reply. Then later, as the forecast worsened. "Seventy-thirty."

Dominic stubbornly refused to accept that the expedition was in jeopardy. He picked out a new ice ax to replace the one he had lost during his glissade to the Col. He was walking in circles in the snow, getting used to the new weight in his hand, when Pasang ran up, howling like a madman. The excited Sherpa grabbed him by the arm and dragged him to the This Way Up mess tent, where a grinning Ethan Zaph handed him the satellite phone.

"The *National Daily* was right! Everest is no place for a thirteen-year-old! And now an innocent Slinky is dead!"

"Nestor!" Dominic cried delightedly. "You're okay!"

THE CLIMB

"Well, sort of," said the voice on the other end of the line. "You know, considering I'm flat on my face with tubes coming out of places I didn't even know I had."

"But you're alive," Dominic insisted.

"Thanks to you, Dominic. That's what I'm calling about. I just want you to know that I'll never forget how you risked your life to save me."

"That's what climbers *do*."

"That's what *you* do," Nestor corrected. "There isn't anyone like you. Not on this planet. If it wasn't for you, I'd still be on that ridge, and we Puerto-Rican Pakistanis don't freeze well. You take care, kid. You're going to be famous someday."

"Safe home, Nestor. We'll miss you." Dominic passed the phone to another ecstatic teammate, and Ethan pulled him aside. "It wasn't me who tipped off the Nepalese about you. You've got to believe me on that."

Dominic nodded slowly. "But you still think I don't belong."

The famous young alpinist shook his head vehemently. "You guys saved our lives! There's something special about you, kid. You more than belong! When the gods made Everest, they probably had you in mind." He put a hand on Dominic's shoulder. "I was wrong and I'm sorry. I'll climb with you any day."

Dominic was melancholy. "I don't think any of us are going to be climbing any time soon."

He stepped out of the tent. A light dusting of powder covered the moraine, belying the violent weather higher up.

*We were at 27,700 feet on Lhotse!* he thought to himself. *Just a quarter mile lower than the Everest summit! We can do this! The top of the world is within reach! All we need is a chance!*

The snow continued, settling on Base Camp and on Dominic's dreams.

THE CLIMB

# ABOUT THE AUTHOR

GORDON KORMAN is the author of more than forty books for children and young adults, including the Island series, *Book One: Shipwreck*, *Book Two: Survival*, and *Book Three: Escape*, as well as *The Chicken Doesn't Skate*, the Slapshots series, and *Liar, Liar, Pants on Fire*. He lives in Long Island with his wife and children, and usually stays close to sea level.